Field of Shamrocks

Where dreams can come true

by

Olga Duckworth

Published by Create Space 2012

Book ID 3928224

Copyright © Olga Duckworth 2012

Olga Duckworth has asserted her right under the Copyright, Design and Patents Act, 1988, to be identified as the author of this book.

This book is a work of fiction. Names and characters are the product of the author's imagination and any resemblance to actual persons, living or dead, is entirely coincidental.

ISBN-13: 978-1478186885

ISBN-10: 1478186887

Field of Shamrocks

by

Olga Duckworth

For Simon, Cayleigh. Colleen & Damien,

Who mean the world to me x

Chapter 1

It was the bleakest, coldest January that had hit Ireland in over twenty years. It was 2010. I had lived all my life in one of the roughest parts of Dublin, Smithfield. Growing up there made you a strong person, you either 'sink or swim' and maybe somehow this had prepared me somewhat. The snow was falling softly outside and there was a deathly silence in the house. My aunt Annie was downstairs with my cousin Fiona, I could hear them talking quietly, hoping I wouldn't hear what they were saying. It was nothing new to what had already been said at the wake yesterday.

"She's still in a state of shock, the poor little mite!" I could hear my aunt saying "It has to be done immediately or it'll be harder for her."

It was the saddest moment in my life. I felt the presence of my mum looking over me and knew she was watching down encouraging me to be strong.

"Come on now Molly, be strong for me" almost hearing her voice for real. The feeling of emptiness and missing her so much really hurt. This was all happening so fast, my stomach ached with not eating for two days and the feeling of being sick would not go away. Sitting on my bed, my little room was decorated in pink and purple floral wallpaper. I was holding a picture frame with a photo of me and my mum, it was taken last St Patrick's Day. We both had shamrocks painted on our faces, and were smiling with sheer happiness, that was a brilliant day, every day with mum was a brilliant day. I was going to miss our little home so much, the council would take it back and re-let it to a new family. Earlier, I had been in my mum's room for a while, just sitting on her empty bed. Someone had already been in and cleared out her wardrobe, all her belongings and even took all the bed linen away. They said this was for the best, for them maybe, but not for me. The smell of her perfume was still lingering in the room. Looking down on the ground where her pretty feet used to tiptoe around, something caught my attention from the corner of my eye, it was her silver charm bracelet she wore all the time. As if a sign from her, I wiped my snuffles on the back of my hand and picked it up and gave it the longest kiss. Putting it on my right wrist like she had always worn it, this will never be taken off I promised myself.

  I knew I should hurry or I would miss the

train, but feeling so lifeless and confused, time did not matter. Hearing footsteps coming up the stairs I tried to finalize my packing when Fiona peered in the doorway of my tiny bedroom.

"Are ye alright Molly?" She asked concerned and put a hand on my shoulder. "Yeah, grand thanks Fi," I replied trying to hold back the tears and deciding what I needed to take with me and what to leave. On my pillow was 'bobo', he was left out to pack last, he was a small rabbit that mum had given me when I was a little girl. He brought back so many memories, a stitched arm for instance, from a tear he got whilst getting off a bus one day as the doors trapped poor bobos arm. Mum had spent hours consoling me whilst she re-stitched it back on. There were so many memories, that's all they are now, memories. I'm only 14 years old and feel like I have to grow up immediately. Silly talk to friends about boyfriends and clothes were none of my concerns anymore.

"I'll send on anything you need or forget, don't worry pet" Fiona said sympathetically. Knowing she was hurt too, I couldn't come to terms with how I was feeling myself to give any comfort back. Fiona helped me carry my suitcases downstairs, I glanced once more at the door into my mum's room, and a memory of her walking towards me with a beautiful smile filled my heart with sorrow. In the hallway downstairs, waiting with her coat on was my aunt Annie.

"Are ye ready child?" she asked, standing stern and stiff. It was her decision to send me away, she thought it would be for the best and it would have been what my mother would have wanted. *'Has she no feelings?'* I was wondering, after all it was her only sister that just died and I hadn't seen her shed one tear.

"Yes, thank you Aunt Annie" I said in a low pitch voice as we walked outside into the softly falling snow. Mum always loved the snow and it was a funny sensation, to feel so close to somebody you knew, yet you would never talk to them again. Trying not to think too much about her, I could see a few neighbours gathered outside to see me off, well-wishers and people who didn't even like us were there.

"God bless ya Molly" and *"Good Luck to ya girl"* were a few comments I could hear, not wanting to look them in the eye, I just kept on walking and gave the odd nod with my head down until I got by the last one. Suddenly feeling extremely sad because of what was happening, I stopped and looked back. People were making their way back to the warmth

of their own homes, some still staring after me. I wasn't looking back to see them, I was looking back at the little cosy council house we lived in for 14 years, that was our home, but not no more.

My mum and I had lived there since I was born. She was lucky enough to get a house from the council when she was pregnant. Her parents had kicked her out of their home when they heard she was expecting, she was only 16 years old at the time. They never had anything to do with her since. She had tried several times to bring me around in hope that there feud could be resolved, but they were stubborn and ignorant and gave her a hard time. They did not approve of my father, he was only a young boy at the time from Connemara in Co. Galway. He now had his own pub in a quiet village called Clada. Even though I had visited my dad on and off throughout my life, and he came to Dublin a couple of times, I still didn't know him properly. I knew the situation; my mum had explained it to me numerous times. She was young and foolish at the time, but had no regrets at the consequences. Hoping that someday my mum and dad would overcome their differences and settle down together, it never evolved. My mum loved Dublin. She was a city girl and my dad was a country boy. Mum had told me that when I was born, dad moved to Dublin but he missed his life in Galway, and she insisted he move back.

My aunt Annie and Fiona walked me to the train station. My aunt bought me my ticket, I noticed it was one way; this was definitely trying to give me a hint.

"Now Molly, listen to me" aunt Annie was fixing my coat and making sure my woolly hat was on correctly. "This is for the best, I know you don't feel this way right now, but there's no point you going to live with us, when your father is there for you." She was looking at me as kindly as she possibly could even though her face could stop a clock! "I know it's sudden, but it'll be for the best." She gave me a tight hug then escorted me onto the train, I suddenly felt extremely lonely and sad and tears started to roll down my cheeks, my mouth was so dry from constantly crying. Sitting at a window seat, Fiona ran to the train's window from the platform. Her eyes were swollen and tears were flowing down her freckled face as she put one hand on the window. I could hear her shout through the glass;

"I'll come and see you soon, I love you Molly" she cried as the train began to roll away.

"I love you too" I choked.

She ran for as long as she could until her hand fell from the window and I could no longer see her. Fellow passengers were looking in curiosity, and trying not to stare but I didn't care. I was leaving my home and my life that I loved behind me. Now here I am, with what feels like a hole in my sad heart, on a train with two suitcases of clothes and memories and with no choice. I was moving to live in Connemara with my dad.

Chapter 2

The train conductor shouted "Eyre Square Galway, final shtop" he made me jump as I woke up; I had drifted off to sleep. Feeling sad sure makes you tired. I grabbed my two cases and got off the train, it was snowing here too and the platforms were all slushy and icy. The cold air made my body shiver as I pulled my woolly hat firmly down over my ears; I looked around to find my dad. At first I could not see him, and then through a crowd in the falling snow, I saw a fair haired man in a quilted navy jacket. He looked right through me, he had tears in his eyes as he walked over to me with his arms out and gave me a long warm hug. Even though he has not been in my life very much, I instantly felt a connection and felt grateful as if a huge burden was being lifted from my shoulders; perhaps I wasn't alone after all.

As I sat in the front seat of his jeep, he didn't quite know what to say but was doing his best.

"Are you ok?" he asked concerned, I just nodded my head and looked out of the window. "When I got back late last night after the funeral, I errrr... got a friend to come around and decorate your new bedroom." He was watching the traffic lights and I could see him biting his bottom lip. He continued by adding "I loved your mother very very much you know." I nodded again, I knew he did. "And I hope you'll be happy here with me," he looked at me seriously "because I love you very very much too."

'Beep Beep' the car horn blew behind us as the lights turned green without my dad realising.

"Thanks" I said with a little smile. "What do you want me to call you?"

He looked a little happier after I spoke, "anything at all my little angel, just as long as it's not too early in the mornin!"

I gave a little laugh, it felt good to finally have something to laugh about. The sadness was still there but I knew mum would want me to feel a bit better.

"Are ye hungry?" he asked, his accent was so different compared to the people in Dublin, it made me chuckle a little.

"A little bit" I replied softly.

"Well good job ye are, coz I made you me specialty..... chicken shtew" he put his hand on my knee "you're going to be alright here, don't worry I'll make sure you are." I felt very comfortable, more than I thought I would have.

"Thanks" I put my hand on his, I wanted him to know I appreciated what it was he was trying to do, and then I said "Thanks Dad." He smiled at me and took my hand and gave it a kiss.

The drive to my new home took about forty minutes from Galway city center. As we entered the village of Clada, every car we met seemed to know my dad. They all waved in the same fashion, one index finger above the steering wheel, and even my dad did the same back. It was starting to get dark and the town's streetlights were coming alight. I could see the large Guinness harp sign lit up outside of my dad's pub, over the entrance was the name "O'Neil's." My mum had made sure I took my dad's name when I was born and she always liked the name Molly, so Molly O'Neil I was. She always had a kind word to say about my dad and never complained that he wasn't around, she just said he was the right guy but the wrong time. She also never got married or had any serious boyfriends, perhaps deep down she thought one day they would get back together, but now I will never know.

As my dad turned into the rear car park

behind his pub, there was only one other car. "Quiet at the minute with all the snow" he said looking at the bleak car park as if reading my mind. "It's much nicer here in the summer."

"I like the snow" I replied. I felt a little bewildered because this was my new home. I was used to the hustle and bustle of Dublin's city center. When I got out of the jeep it seemed so silent. Dad brought my bags in through the back entrance, there was a stairs leading up to the living quarters and then a door with 'BAR' written on it.

"So do you want to settle in? Or have a look around? It's all changed since you were here last." He was holding my two cases and looked as if he wanted me to see the bar first so I nodded towards the bar.

Inside it was cosy and warm, there was a roaring fire spitting from the wall to the right and beside it was a long mahogany bar with gleaming beer pumps. A woman who looked around thirty years old, popped up from behind the bar when she heard us come in, she was eating a packet of peanuts which she tried to get rid of quickly, my dad just smiled and said "How are ye Kerry?."

"Not a bother Martin, and yerself?" she replied. She was a pretty girl with dark hair and was wearing a black top and pants, she blushed slightly whilst talking to my dad, and probably the heat of the fire I thought. "And this must be Molly" she added, "It's lovely to meet you, I'm Kerry" she stepped around from the bar and came towards me with a warm hug

"I'm so sorry to hear about your mother", she seemed very nice and very sincere "It must be such a shock for you."

"Thanks" I said. I looked around and there was only one man with a big pot belly sitting at the end of the bar, my dad walked over to the guy and gave him a pat on the back.

"Well Mick, how's she now?" asked my dad casually.

"Arra not two bad atall Marty and yourself?" said the guy who was clearly not on his first pint of Guinness I thought. And what language was he speaking? He spoke so fast it was hard to know exactly what he just said!

"Ahh sure grand, grand. Let me introduce you to my daughter," said dad as he put his arm out for me to join him "this is Molly" he said proudly. I knew by the way he introduced me that he felt proud to have me there.

"Hiya" I stretched my hand out to shake Mick's.

"God Bless ya child, God Bless ya, you've been through a terrible time, but your daddy here is over the moon to have you with him." Mick's voice was croaky and wheezy like he smoked too much.

"Thanks, I'm happy to be here too." I was telling the truth, I was grateful to have him, he may not have been around before but at least he's here now.

"Can I get you a drink" offered Mick

"Maybe later," said my dad who sensed I was probably tired and wanted to get settled in.

"Thank you, but I think I'll get my bags upstairs" shyly I began to walk over to the door.

"Catch you later honey" said Kerry from behind the bar; she was now busy polishing the shiny bar pumps. I gave her a little wave then headed out into the hallway to the stairs that lead to the living quarters. It was different to when I was here last with my mum, it was all redecorated and very clean and tidy.

Upstairs was all open plan, the floors were all covered in a cosy cream carpet, a comfy living room with a large television and brown leather settees, adjoining this room was the kitchen with a breakfast counter that looked into the living room, my dad pointed out a few things to me then showed me to my new room.

"Now when I said I had it redecorated last night, well, our decor man is Mick, the chap downstairs, so my apologies in advance if it's not to your liking." He opened the door and waited for me to enter "we can always change it this week if you want."

"No, no, it's lovely thank you" I could see a single bed under the window, the walls were covered in pink heart wallpaper, it was a little childish but I wasn't going to say anything. The cover on my bed had 'My Little Pony' and a matching lamp on a bedside table, along with a picture frame, I walked over and discovered a photo of my mum when she was young with my dad. They both looked so happy; I had never seen that picture before. I felt so sad when I saw her young face but still had that protective feeling over myself to be strong.

"That was taken a long time ago," said dad who sat on the bed and waited for me to do the same. "It was taken when she was expecting you, I thought all my Christmas's had come at once."

"Why didn't you stay in Dublin? Or why didn't she move here?" I was still not quite sure why they were apart so much.

"Well, tis like this.... your grandparents didn't approve of the situation, and your mother always said I reminded her too much of all the arguments. I guess she just thought it was best for me not to be around," he looked very sad; I could tell he was sensitive and probably did what he was told all his life.

"I wish you had been around" I tried to hold in my tears but they just caught up on me, I hadn't cried since morning time and now needed to do it again. My dad put his warm arms around me and held me close, he rocked me backwards and forwards, kissing my head, he started to sing *'Molly Malone'* to me softly, my mum always sang that to me when I was little any time I was upset or hurt.

"It must have been terrible for you" he said as his glossy eyes looked into mine "when your Aunt Anne told you."

I hadn't spoken about it to anyone but I felt I needed to get it off my chest. I looked at the photo of when she was young, only two years older than I am now, she must have been strong to make the decisions she had made. I swallowed and dried up my tears a little and began to explain to dad what had happened.

"I had come home from school, the snow was really bad and I was thinking about what movie me and mum should go see at the weekend. When I got home Aunt Anne was in the doorway and she was just standing sternly staring at me as I got closer, I thought 'ohh no'… She's found cigarettes me and Fiona had" I looked at dad who raised an eyebrow "we were only trying them out" I assured him with a grin. "then when I went inside Fiona was crying and so were a few others who were there, I asked where mum was?" I stopped talking and relived the moment in my head. "Aunt Anne just sat me down and said 'there's been an accident'. It's funny you know" I said "it was the worst thing to hear but before she said what she said, I actually thought about it." I slipped onto the floor off my bed and put my head in my knees and began to cry, dad slid down beside me.

"You don't have to tell me pet" he had his arms around me giving me a tight hug. I wiped my face and looked at him.

"No, it's ok." I continued "She told me there was an accident on the bus my mum took from work, it over turned on an icy road and there was nothing anyone could do. She was the only person who died, everyone else survived" I was crying harder than ever and my voice began to rise and I couldn't help myself as I wailed "Why her? WHY??" I was asking my dad who was also in floods of tears, not knowing what to tell me he just sat patiently.

It was about an hour later as my dad sat with me on the floor together, holding me and telling me everything would be alright. His shirt was soaking from my tears and his own. He told me all the wonderful things he loved about mum and how pretty she was when he first laid eyes on her. As we talked and talked I then realised that my dad wasn't a stranger at all, he was just as close to me as mum was, only I never got to know him properly before. He then went into the kitchen to heat up the 'shtew' as he called it. I unpacked my belongings and took out bobo and gave him a long hug and whispered *"we'll be ok...."* I put him on top of my pillow and smiled at my new room as I left to join dad in the kitchen.

Chapter 3

It was spring. All the snow had finally gone. It was a Saturday morning and I woke up early, mainly because the cows in the field behind the pub were mooing really loudly. In Dublin I always used to sleep in late on a Saturday, the noise of buses, cars, horns blowing never bothered me, but now these guys outside where getting on my wick! Every morning around 6.00am they would start to *"Mooooo,"* and then Bill, who I now know, is the farmer who owns those annoying cows, parks in our car park and re-fills his tank of water that's attached to his tractor, leaving the engine running which is right under my bedroom window! Of course my dad would never say no to him, he's too nice for his own good I keep thinking.

    I walked over to my window sleepily, in a long pink nightgown I peered out, as soon as I did Bill looked up, gave me a huge wave and shouted "Morning Molly, hope I haven't woken ya." I just gave him a wave back then made my way into our living room, dad always hears me getting up and jumped out of bed himself. He opened his door with his dressing gown on and came over to give me a kiss.

"Did you sleep alright pet?" he asked as he headed towards the kitchen to make me breakfast.

"Yeah fine thanks, until Bill woke me" I tried to let him see that it's a bit of a joke but he just laughed a little bit.

"Yeah Bill's gas alright, I think he's married to them cows, although can't say I blame him, his wife's an awful woman. She came into the pub one night and hit him on the head with her handbag and dragged him home, doesn't like me at all, thinks I feed him too much drink."

"Kerry told me that story" I said as I sat on one of the high stools at the breakfast bar.

"So what do you want to do today?" he asked as he took out some eggs from the fridge, "scrambles alright?" he added, giving him a yes nod he continued on "I've to see a man about a dog."

"What? We're getting a dog?" suddenly I felt a bit excited.

"No, no, sorry pet, I shouldn't have got your hopes up like that, no I've to go to Craglea to see a fella about a pool table I might get for downstairs, what do you think about that?" he looked at me for a reaction to his new idea.

"yeah cool" I wasn't really into snooker or pool but I just wanted to seem enthusiastic.

"I thought maybe it might attract a younger crowd, maybe you could make a few new friends" he said.

"I'm ok, stop worrying. School's fine I'm making new friends everyday." I didn't really like to tell him that I hardly spoke to anyone, only because they all seemed to be in their own little groups and not very inviting towards me.

"Well I'll go have a look anyways, do you want to come with me?" he was buttering the toast, pouring me orange juice all at the one time.

"Thanks, but I might go for a cycle on that bike outside if that's ok?" The scrambles, toast and juice were put in front of me. He's quite a good cook I was thinking, poor mum always burnt the toast, over did the scrambles, but still, they would taste great too.

"Good idea, get some fresh air into ya" he sat down beside me and started to eat. "If you go that-a way" he said pointing towards one end of town "you'll be on the Galway road to Ballymuck.

And if you go this-a way" again pointing to the other end of town "it's the Galway road... to Galway," he smiled at his own jokes. There was one thing about him, he always had a lot of jokes.

"Ballymuck it is then" I said as I finished off the plate. "Thanks dad." I stood up and gave him a kiss on the cheek.

"Molly" he said as I was walking towards my room "I'm very proud of you," he was looking a little sad at me, I knew why, he missed her as much as I did too, and I couldn't stop missing her, "I'm very proud of the way you're handling yourself, your mother has done a fantastic job," he gave me a wink and I turned towards my room. When I shut the door I couldn't help filling up with tears again, as I slid down onto the floor and put my head in my knees and cried as quietly as I could so dad wouldn't hear. He was so nice, did everything for me, got me anything I wanted and always helped me with my homework, but the love for my mum would never ever go away, I fiddled with my charm bracelet and had to keep thinking to myself '*be strong.*'

When I went downstairs my dad had the bike out, he was checking the tyres, testing the breaks, getting the seat the right height...

"Dad stop fussing, I'm only going for some fresh air, not the Tour -De-France!" I said as I took the bike from him.

"Sorry pet, I know I'm fussing, but this old thing hasn't been out for a while so just giving it a quick check" he was studying the bike as I got on it "Take it aezy won't you pet".

"Go inside, you're embarrassing me in front of the cows." With that I headed out onto the road, left or right, left or right, can't remember what dad told me... right I thought quickly and it didn't take long before I was out of the town and into the countryside.

It was a beautiful day, it was still a little cold but there wasn't a cloud in the sky, as I cycled along the road I felt free, all the fields around me were protected with little stone walls, I was heading towards some donkeys who watched me get closer towards them as I struggled up a hill, they were staring at me as if they were taking bets, 'will she make it, or will she push the bike' as I got closer to them I shouted "How-are-ye" at the top of my lungs. I had a quick check to see if anyone was around but luckily not. The donkeys didn't budge or blink an eyelid, I decided to stop and give them a little pat, they looked harmless I thought. Then suddenly in the field beyond them, that was a darker shade of green than any other field around, galloped a beautiful grey horse. He was prancing his legs up really high with his tail lifted high in the air, he looked towards me and gave a huge loud snort, I could see his breath exhale out sharply through his nostrils. I looked around to see what could be startling him but I couldn't see anyone, or anything else for miles in either direction, it was just me and three donkeys that looked as if they were going to have a nap. The horse whinnied at me, it was a very high pitch whinny. I'm no equine expert but he seemed to be distressed. I put my bike down on the grass verge and walked along the road, the horse in the field behind the donkeys walked along the inside of his wall too in the same direction as I was going. I stopped and watched him. He stopped and watched me. I walked on a bit further. He did the same.

  I decided to go say hello and get a closer look, the donkeys were staring at my bike, so I didn't feel that I was in any great danger by entering their field. I climbed over the stone wall and landed in the wet dew grass the other side, walking towards the grey horse my feet were getting soaked and the end of my jeans were saturated in seconds. The grey horse stared at me, his ears were pricked pointing towards me and his eyes were reading every move I made. As I walked down the hill towards his field and got closer, I noticed him twitch and his withers flicker. My only knowledge of horses were the ones I watched in Smithfield market in Dublin, I was always fascinated by them but never had been alone in a situation like this before. My heart began to beat quicker as I moved slower in my final steps towards him. As I got closer I stretched my hand up to touch him, with that he turned extremely fast and with a loud whinny he galloped across the field way down the hill to the other side of the field. He pranced around again like before, breathing very loudly, steam snorting out of his flaring nostrils, tail up high and stretched out. *'Well I'm not going to the other end of that field'* I thought to myself, *'silly horse'*. I stood there for a long while just watching him, he was the most beautiful creature I had ever seen in my life. He looked lonely maybe that's why he's so unsettled. My feet were cold and wet so I decided to go home and have a hot bath. Walking back up the field, the three donkeys had turned around to watch me, probably making another bet I thought, the hill was so steep I was out of shape when I got to the top. The wall was no longer a little stone wall, on this side it was huge, how am I going to get over it now I thought. I put one foot on a groove of the wall and tried to pull myself up, it was no use, my trainers were so wet they couldn't grip. *'Ohhh good God'* I thought, *'I'm trapped in a field with three sarcastic donkeys'*, there's something you don't say every day! I walked along the wall to where the donkeys stood and found the ground was a little higher. "Could have told me" I said to the three guys. I tried again with one foot on the wall and with that, I managed to pull myself up and over. *'Thank God for that!'*

    I said my goodbyes to the donkeys and started to head home, I looked back to the field with the fabulous grey. He was following my every move. I kept looking behind as I cycled along the road home. Still, he kept watching. A feeling of excitement and adrenalin rushed through my body as I kept thinking about him and the image of his power over me kept coming into my head. I wanted to tell my dad but I was afraid he would go mad if he knew what I just did, so I decided to keep it to myself.

    That night at home the bar was filling below, I could hear the crowd's laughter and some music playing. My dad had popped upstairs a few times to check in on me, he had rented a video for me to watch, I wasn't really concentrating on it, so I decided to change from my slippers to trainers and go downstairs. I didn't usually go down but tonight I felt I wanted to.

When I walked into the bar, the room was filled with locals and tourists, Kerry was busy behind the bar pulling pints, she caught my eye and gave me a little wave then went over to my dad and whispered in his ear. Dad looked straight at me with a huge smile "Molly come over here pet" he shouted through the crowd. I walked over shyly as he came from behind the bar and arranged a high stool for me to sit on. "What'll ye have?" he asked me as I sat up on the stool. There was a line of people sitting at the bar, they all stared at me, some smiled and nodded, others just watched as if to see if anything amazing was going to happen.

"Errr can I have a coke please?" I asked "and some hot nuts?"

"Your wish is my command my dearest" said my dad as he skipped to the other side of the bar to get me my drink and nuts.

From the other end of the bar, an elderly man shouted up "O'Neil, where's me flaming pint?"

"Be with you in a minute Johnny, important customer down here you know" he looked at me with a wink, the man who he called Johnny was getting impatient and starting to mumble some swear words. "Ladies present Johnny, watch your tone" added my dad. Johnny was not happy with the situation and just sulked.

As I sat drinking my coke and nibbling on my nuts, I couldn't help thinking about the grey horse I saw earlier, he was so majestic and so beautiful, I couldn't get him out of my head.

"Whatcha thinking about?" asked my dad as he pulled pints of Guinness and whizzed around the bar, it was only him and Kerry working but they made a good team.

"Nothing" I lied and sipped my coke, "I might go for another cycle tomorrow if that's alright?" I asked.

"Course tis pet" he answered as he gave someone their change, "as long as you don't go far."

"Just the same as today" I said.

For a minute I thought my dad looked really cool, but then he tried to do a Tom Cruise impression from the movie Cocktail and dropped a bottle that smashed all over the floor. Kerry was telling him off for being so stupid.

I loved reading all the signs that were around the bar, one said *"Free Beer Tomorrow"* another *"God invented Whiskey, to keep the Irish from ruling the world"*. A man and a woman, who were next to me at the bar, were watching me read the signs.

"So you must be Martin's daughter" said the man next to me "I'm Sean and this is Rose" he put out his hand for me to do the same, he shook my hand and nearly stopped the blood circulating it was such a hard hand shake.

"Hiya" I replied, relieved when he let go, I was checking my hand to see if it wasn't crushed when his wife Rosie spoke.

"I'm sorry for your loss dear, but you're a lucky girl ya know" she nodded towards my dad, "He never stops talking about you, let me give you a little advice" and she turned to Sean "put your hands over your ears you" she shouted crossly to him, surprisingly he did just that, jeeez I thought, don't ever mess with a Connemara woman! She leaned closer and whispered in my ear "There are only two tragedies in life: one is not getting what one wants, and the other is getting it..... Oscar Wilde, clever boy!" she then let Sean put his hands down and she sat back to continue her drink, strange I thought, yet in some ways exactly how I felt.

"So Rosie" said my dad "How's life treating ye both?"

"Well now Martin, all is grand apart from himself here" she pointed to her husband who stopped drinking and looked at her in surprise.

"What have I done now?" asked Sean.

"It's what you haven't done!" she exclaimed "Isn't that right Kerry?" she looked over to Kerry for some backup.

"That's exactly right Rosie" said Kerry with a big smile. I couldn't make out what was going on and then Rosie told Sean to cover his ears again.

"When you get a little older and finally find the man you want to spend the rest of your life with…… think twice…. then twice more! That's my advice to any woman!" Rosie gave me a nod and left me in bewilderment as I looked at Kerry for some help, she then added "And as for Kerry and Martin…" but she was cut off by Kerry very sharply.

"As for me and your dad" said Kerry who looked flushed all of a sudden "anyone would think we're married with the arguments we have, but it's only the work that has us like this" she gave Rosie a stare and then asked me "How was your cycle today luv?"

"Good," I replied. I wanted to mention the horse but thought I'd better not.

I finished off my drink and nuts feeling tired, some more people came into the bar, I wasn't that interested in making new friends or getting to know too many people, even though my dad proudly introduced me to everyone that came through the door, so I said my goodbyes to Sean and Rosie and headed back upstairs for bed. For the first time in weeks I went to bed holding the picture of my mum and dad, not crying myself to sleep but smiling at them instead. I kept thinking about what the woman in the bar said to me earlier and was trying to make head or tail of it. Tomorrow after Bill wakes me no doubt, I'll go see that horse again. I closed my eyes and drifted into a deep restful sleep.

Chapter 4

All I can say is, 'Thanks Bill!' as I jumped out of bed and looked to see what the weather was like. Bill, my personal alarm clock, waved from below, and today I gave him a smile and got dressed quickly. As I walked out of my room dad was already in the kitchen, he was yawning and rubbing the back of his neck. He didn't hear me approach with the kettle whistling, as he poured boiling water into his cup he jumped as he suddenly saw me "jeeez Molly I didn't hear ya, I'm still asleep" he looked extremely tired I thought. He walked around and gave me a kiss on my head like always.

"Rough night dad?" I asked as he returned back into the kitchen. I sat on a stool and tucked my jeans into my socks.

"Could say that, I hope it wasn't too loud on you? Did you sleep alright?" he was always worrying about me.

"I slept good thanks" I said honestly. "I'm not that hungry actually, can I go for a cycle and have something when I come back?"

"What? you're going out

now?....phhheeeww, suppose, just you be extra careful... you promise?" he was looking after me as I jumped off the stool, grabbed an apple and walked over to the door to put my wellies on.

"I'll be fine, I just really like cycling" I said to him as I finished getting ready before going downstairs.

"Good, good, enjoy yourself pet" he said bringing his tea towards his bedroom, "ohh and Molly, by the way" he added before he went into his room "you're the first cyclist I ever saw who loves wearing wellies" he raised an eyebrow as if he knew I was up to something and gave me a little smile before going back to bed for a while.

I raced down the stairs and jumped on my bike, Bill was still filling his tank up "morning Bill" I shouted as I tore away onto the main street to head out of town.

"Top of the mornin to ya young Molly" I could hear him shout, I thought only souvenir leprechauns said that!

I was peddling as fast I could, and as soon as I was at the bottom of the hill I recognised the field. It was definitely a darker green and dotted in the distance was the grey horse. He was grazing then suddenly he looked up and stared right in the direction I was coming from, he's got good ears I thought. The three donkeys had moved from where I left them yesterday and were grazing also, they looked over one by one. Start betting boys I thought as I stood up on my pedals and leaned as far forward as I could and peddled with all my strength, nearly there I thought, I wasn't going to give in to the pain and strain on my legs and body. Finally I was up the hill and stopped to get my breath back, I could hardly breathe and the cold morning air made me cough. My bike fell as I leaned on the stone wall and watched the horse. This time I jumped over where it was lower, and I was prepared - no wet feet today! I walked by the donkeys who weren't too interested in me but more interested in their grass. The grey horse watched me closely as if I was a threat to him, he stood in the middle of 'his' field and didn't move an inch, it was like he was frozen. The morning air was crisp and I could see him breathing, his breath exhaling slowly. I carefully climbed over his wall. it was his territory now. Walking slower this time towards him, I had a plan.... as I got closer, putting my hand in my pocket and produced an apple, I held it out flat and without saying any words I walked slowly and calmly towards him. I was looking at him straight in the eyes, and then suddenly he moved, he took one step towards me. I stopped and stood still not knowing what to do next. He stood still also, so I took one more step towards him, with that he turned and fled away kicking soil into my face, I felt humiliated and cheated. This horse was messing with my head and it infuriated me, I gave a shout in anger and threw the apple towards his direction, he galloped to the other end, then up along one side of the field, I ran after him like a crazy woman, I was mad at him for not wanting to know me, I was mad because I had lost my mum, I was mad because I loved my dad and felt guilty towards my beautiful mum for feeling that way, I waved my arms and he galloped and galloped around me, he was trying to make a circle around me, I pushed him away and made him go in the opposite direction. I was so upset. He still galloped and galloped but I noticed his circle around me was getting closer and smaller. For some reason, the woman in the bar last night came into my head what she said... something about 'not getting what you want, then getting it'.... I don't know why but for some reason I knew this horse was in some ways just like me, maybe he lost his mum to? I calmed down and watched him as he galloped around. I gave the odd wave of my hands in the air as if to tell him 'you're in my territory, not the other way around'. I could see his ear that was closest to me turned and listened to every move I made. He looked a little more relaxed, his gallop changed to a canter, he moved so majestically. I was suddenly in tune with him again. He lowered his neck and slowed down into a trot, he was licking and chewing his lips, I followed him as he circled around me, the circles getting smaller and smaller. I kept chasing him away until I suddenly stopped and looked to the ground...... Silence....... I was scared but didn't want to move. I stood completely still like a statue and then I heard him move, he walked confidently towards me, he didn't hesitate he walked right over to my right shoulder and nudged me with his muzzle. My heart was in my mouth, I was never so terrified and still didn't look at him in the eye as I turned towards him, I rubbed his nose, it felt thick and soft and his furlock felt damp, moving my hands up his head slowly. He flapped his solid ears through my hands before I softly rubbed his neck. He stood completely still, he gave the odd swish of his tail, and lowered his head around my body, I rubbed his neck as if giving him a hug, and I was still terrified yet completely safe. I rubbed my hands along his back, then along his hind quarters and then ran my hand down along his tail. I walked under his neck and did the same the other side, he had a small cut on his hind right leg. I then returned to face him and turned my back and walked away, at first I heard nothing, then the soaking grass behind me made a noise, he was following me! I turned left, he followed, I turned right, and he followed. I stopped, he stopped. I walked backwards and so did he. Then for the first real time I looked him in the eyes, he lowered his head and let me rub him again, I played with his ears and stroked his large cheek bones and as he made chewing noises with his mouth. I looked around the field in search of the apple I threw at him before, there it was.... I walked over to get it, and of course he followed.... I picked the apple up and held it out for him, he stretched down and took a big bite, he seems relaxed now and not at all the wild horse he was about ten minutes ago. "Hi" I said to him softly, he chewed on the apple and was looking for more, I gave a giggle as his muzzle buried into my jacket pocket to see if I had anything else to give him.

I spent some more time with him walking around and getting him to follow me, I even tried running and he trotted behind me, once or twice he got a little over excited and broke into a canter and kicked up his two hind legs high into the air. I had never felt like this before, I was so content it felt like I should put him on the back of my bike and take him home.... 'OH no' I thought, I better get back or dad will be worried. I gave my new found friend a kiss in the middle of his forehead "I'll come see you tomorrow" I said to him, he looked a little sad "ohh feckit, I have school..... I'll think of something, so don't go anywhere" I hugged him once more and ran to the wall to climb over it, he followed me to the wall also. "I'll have to give you a name" he was looking at me and I knew he didn't want me to leave. I was climbing over the stone wall when I looked on the ground and saw rushes and rushes of shamrocks lining the edge of the field "Shamrocks" I said as I looked at him. It suited him I thought.... "See you tomorrow Shamrocks" and with that I made my way to my bike, passing the donkeys who looked on in awe "do you awwww, do you awwww, do you awwwways look like that?" I chuckled at my own joke, may as well I thought because these three guys won't.

I free wheeled all the way down the hill and kept looking back at Shamrocks to make sure he was ok. He was watching me the whole time until I got out of sight again.

Back home I went straight into the bar, my dad and Kerry were sitting down going over some figures.

"Here she is" exclaimed my dad, "I was about to set up a search party, you alright?"

"Yeah grand, I just got carried away and went for a long cycle in this lovely weather" I said trying to sound convincing.

"It's freezin out, I think you're mad" said Kerry as she touted at her calculator.

"Dad, I went as far as three donkeys on the Galway road" I pointed in the direction I went. "Well I was wondering, there was a grey horse in a field behind them, who owns him?"

"Well now let me see" said dad putting a pen behind his ear, "so you're telling me, you cycled as far as three donkeys and want to know who owns the grey horse in the field behind them?".

"Yes" I was all ears, I couldn't believe it was this easy to find out.

"Molly my dear", he said as he leaned towards me "this is Connemara, there are over 10,000 grey horses scattered all over the land..... And donkeys multiply around here like rabbits"

I felt devastated all of a sudden, he knows everyone, why doesn't he know this I thought... I sat back in my chair a little sulky and folded my arms as my dad took the pen from behind his ear and looked at the sheet of figures in front of him.

"Walsh's horse" said Kerry who didn't even look up from her calculator. She got my attention immediately.

"What?" asked my dad looking at her with a confused expression on his face.

"The grey horse.... in a field behind three donkeys.... that's Walsh's" she said as she looked up from her work. "Molly was asking about...."

"I know what you mean, but how do you know which horse?" said dad getting aggravated.

Kerry looked at me questioningly "up the steep hill yeah?" I nodded "three donkeys and a mad grey horse flying around in the field behind?"

"Yeah that's him, that's the one" I said excitedly.

"Why do you need to know?" asked dad.

"I was just wondering... who's Walsh?" I was suddenly interested in knowing who people were now.

"Tommy Walsh, he owns a stud farm, comes in here every Friday for a few pints" Kerry said as she tutted again trying to redo what she wanted to get done on the calculator.

"Are you up to something?" asked dad who now looked at me as if I had done something wrong.

"Noooo, I was just curious, the horse looks so lonely and sweet" I replied.

"Sweet! if that's what you call sweet my dear, I would hate to taste your cooking! That horse is lupo, he's in a field by himself because Walsh couldn't get anyone to ride him" said Kerry.

I thought it best not to tell them what had just happened, I didn't want to cause any trouble, plus I knew where I was going to go tomorrow, Shamrocks was left alone in this world, so was I. I found my dad and Shamrocks has found me.

Chapter 5

As I sat by the window at the back of the class room, I couldn't wait for the bell to ring. To save time I had already put my blazer in my schoolbag and had visited my locker before the final class. The room was so stuffy and a few of the others were passing notes to one another, I knew none would be passed to me, they seemed to joke about what they all did over the weekend and what they have planned for the weekend coming. The classes most popular girl Roisin was all me, me, me as she had everyone following her around like lambs, I couldn't care less about her and this annoyed her! I had been feeling so sad and sorrowful for mum, it didn't bother me in the least that I didn't have any new friends.

As I looked outside the window once more I knew the bell was going to ring any second, there in the car park, always on time, was my dad's jeep.

As the bell rang everyone jumped up and rushed into the hallways. It was a ritual everyone seemed to do, after the last class, go to their lockers and hang around while they talked about boys and stuff. I had other things on my mind.... I ran out of the school as fast as I could and jumped into the jeep beside my dad.

"Hey dad" I said as I stretched over to give him a kiss.

"How are ye pet" he said "you're out very quick, are you settling in ok?" he looked genuinely concerned.

"Yeah of course I am" I reassured him.

"Because if you needed more time, then we can talk about it" he started his engine and pulled away from the car park.

He looked at me sadly knowing what I was thinking "Actually, I wanted to have a little chat to you about something, now maybe this is none of my business, but you're a young woman, and if there's anything you need to tell me, or ask me about… you know…" he scratched his head and looked out the window and added "or if there's anything you need to know about you know what…. Or anything you want to ask about you know what…. I hope you know you can do that..."

"Dad... I'm 14 years old, and the you know what's I've had since I was 12. I wear a you know what since this year and ohh yeah.... I know how things are made" I looked at his shocked face and started to laugh, it was funny and so simple to tease him! He looked embarrassed but just started the engine and said:

"Right then, so that's that little chat sorted, glad I could help!"

"Don't worry dad, I know I can ask Kerry anything if I needed to, if that's alright with you?" He looked at me with a nod.

"Great, great, if there's ever anything that Kerry doesn't know about "you know what" you can come to me.... as long as it's not about… boys… or kissing and stuff!"

I chuckled at him. "Ohhh, stop worrying I'm fine! Can I go for a cycle again when I get home?"

"You can, but only if you're back in half an hour, okay?" he instructed sternly.

"Okay okay" I replied. *'Yes'* I thought, *'going to see my likkle Shamrocks again'.*

When we got home, I was changed and out the door as quick as you could say 'Jack Robinson', I cycled as fast as I could possibly go, on approach to the hill I gathered up my speed as much as possible and it certainly helped.... I flew up it, still out of breath and exhausted, I looked beyond my three friends and there in the field watching me was Shamrocks.

    I hoped he would remember me and not run away like he had done before, as I had anticipated, he walked towards the stone wall from his side as I reached the wall from my side. After climbing over I gave him a pat all over and took and apple out of my pocket "you like these huh?" I asked him. I walked around and he followed again, then I ran a little with him following me, turning fast left then right, he was excited and played with me. He was careful not to get too close or make me feel uncomfortable. I was soon out of breath and I walked over to the stone wall and jumped up on it for a rest, he rested his head on my lap with his chin on my legs, I stroked his beautiful face all over and kissed it several times. "I wish mum was here to meet you Shamrocks" I told him. "She died in January" I started to think about it again, it went over and over in my head all the time but I couldn't bring myself to say it out loud. Shamrocks just waited patiently and didn't move while I sat there thinking about my mum. "Well, I better get going or dad will be wondering where I am" he still didn't budge "same time tomorrow?" I asked him, and then put my hands under his cheek and made a silly voice for him *"yesh Molly, and don't forget the apple"*. I gave him one last hug and jumped down off the wall and walked by the three donkeys on my way to get my bike. "All the best lads" I shouted at them, they didn't answer. As I cycled away I kept checking over my shoulder to see him, he followed me again until he was out of sight.

      I visited Shamrocks every single day, rain, hale, sleet, snow or sunshine.... I never missed one day. During the week I was only allowed 30 minutes after school and on Saturdays and Sundays I went first thing in the morning, sometimes twice on the one day! I always brought him an apple and now when he saw me coming on my bike from the bottom of the steep hill he would whinny in excitement and gallop around until I got closer, sometimes I would tell him off for being over excited "you could slip and break a leg" I would tell him but he didn't seem to listen, I was so excited to see him every day too, my dad was happy that I enjoyed cycling so much, there was a problem one day when he asked could he come with me, so I told him Kerry was looking for him in the bar and when he came out I had already gone. Another day he said why didn't I go in the other direction, so I waved my goodbye and when he was out of sight turned and raced back in the direction towards Shamrocks.

Everything was going well until one day after running around with Shamrocks for a while I stood up on the wall to see how tall he was, he walked around and stood parallel to me with his back beside me. "Ohhhhh no, I'm not that stupid!" I said to him. I tried to push him away so I could sit back down on the wall, but he wouldn't move. "You're being stubborn now Shamrocks" I said to him boldly. But he still wouldn't move. "Right.... fine, fine" I exclaimed as I rubbed down his back "don't you dare do anything silly" I warned him. Then holding onto his mane I swung my right leg over his back, he was warm and very comfortable. It was the first time I had ever sat on a horse, I felt like John Wayne! I didn't have a clue what to do, but this felt so cool, I wasn't one bit scared now, maybe if he moves that will change I thought. He just stood there and never flickered, so I nudged him with my heels a little bit and he walked forward. The movement was rocky but comfortable and I felt confident enough, so after a little while I nudged him a little more with my heels, I held onto his long grey mane as he progressed into a trot, "easy boy" I said nervously, his trot was bouncy and threw my body forward which wasn't comfortable at all! I tried leaning forward more like jockeys do on the TV but this was making my balance worse and I nearly slipped off down the right side of him so I tried sitting up straighter, this was better I thought. Shamrocks kept trotting along the boundary of the wall which I was grateful for as it was level enough. I could sit to the beat of his rhythm it went one two... one two... one two... I used the seat of my bottom for balance and let my legs fall softly around his belly. I still had a tight grip on his mane and could feel the wind blowing through my long blonde hair.

    I squeezed a little with my right leg and moved my left leg a little further back, and suddenly Shamrocks turned to the right "Wow, well done boy" I stretched down to give him a cuddle but nearly lost my balance again, my heart jumped right through my throat and nearly out my mouth! I quickly regained my balance and sat to his rhythm again and decided to try it again, this time I squeezed with my left leg and put my right leg a little further back, "Sweet" I exclaimed, Shamrocks had turned left! I was really enjoying this. I slowed the movement of my seat down and so did Shamrocks and finally relaxed down into a walk and then a halt.

    "Well done Shamrocks, that was sooo cool"

I leaned forward and gave him a huge hug around his neck and swung my right leg over his back as I landed with a 'thud'.

"That was sooo cool" I was on such a high, I had never sat on a horse before and now I trotted and turned. I didn't know what else to do but I was over the moon with the feeling I had. I realised I had been here far too long, so I had to excuse myself quickly. Shamrocks looked a little sad to me, but I had to go or I would get into trouble.

"I'll see you early tomorrow" I shouted back to him, he whinnied after me, I think he was saying "just keep bringing me an apple".

I cycled home as fast as I could, the wind was blowing in my face making my cheeks quiver back towards my ears. I was trying to concentrate because I was going so fast but all I could do was think about Shamrocks, *"I want to do it again"* is all that I was thinking.

As I entered into the village of Clada I could see my dad's pub. Outside parked was a Garda car and a Guard standing at his door talking on his CB radio, I wondered what could be wrong and then I saw my dad who was passing frantically up and down the pavement. I could hear his shout "It's not like her, she's never away this long and I've checked everywhere"

"Sometimes children run away after an incident like a family death" said the guard from the passenger side of his car. Just then he saw me approach and my dad followed his stare.

"MOLLY" he shouted out loud and ran to grab me off my bike. He put his arms around me and hugged me "I thought I was losing you too" he took my head in his hands "are you all right?" he was crying and very upset.

"I'm fine, why what's wrong?" I was confused, had something happened?

"You've been gone two hours, and I drove up and down these roads searching for you, with no sign of you anywhere, where were you?" he was not happy and I didn't know what to say.

"Just cycling dad, like I always do" I said. I was feeling funny about not telling him about Shamrocks but I couldn't.

"Well you're not going again" he took the bike from me and wheeling it away I felt a sudden rush of panic, what did he mean? He can't do this!

"Sorry Tom" he said to the Garda "I'll get to the bottom of this and thanks again."

"No problem Martin" said the guard as he put on his blue hat "I'll be around tonight might pop in and make sure everything's alright" he gave my dad a wink which was returned with a knowing nod from my dad. In real language this meant that Tom will call after hours and have a few free Jameson's!

I was walking after dad and not feeling happy, I did nothing wrong here..

"What do you mean? I love my cycles, please dad don't take the bike away" I pleaded to him for the first time in my life.

"I'm sorry pet, but you're all I have in this world and I'm not losing you" he said sternly.

"You can't do this" I shouted, tears started to pour out of my eyes, I was feeling so cheated.

He dropped the bike to the ground and walked back to me, he looked frustrated "I've drove up and down these roads looking for you, and you were no place to be seen. So I don't know where you have been going for months now, so that's it. No more bike. And I demand you tell me the truth about where you go and who you're with!"

I was crying so much but he didn't seem to be caring, what about Shamrocks I thought, what will happen now? He was the one thing in my life that I believed in. I didn't know what to say so I ran past my dad and into the pub and upstairs into my room. I fell onto the bed sobbing my heart out. Mum would never have punished me like this, and I don't think I'd done anything wrong. I felt destroyed again, is there nothing left in my life to live for? I could hear my dad call my name telling me dinner was ready. I wasn't hungry, I didn't want anything to eat and I didn't want to see him. I lay on my bed holding Bobo sobbing into his damp ears, I changed my clothes and got under the covers, I held the picture of my mum and stared at it until the room was completely dark.

    I woke up to the sound of Bill and his tractor as usual. I didn't jump out of bed as I always did I just lay there feeling sorry for myself. What have I to get up for now I was thinking. I rolled over and hugged Bobo when I heard a light knock on the door.

    "Molly, can I come in?" Dad was talking quietly; I didn't answer him and closed my eyes to pretend I was asleep incase the door opened. I heard his feet move away from the door and into the kitchen. I could hear him filling up the kettle and rustling around. I stared at the photo of mum on my bedside table and wished she was here again, feeling lost and alone I didn't believe that I would ever find happiness. I thought about Shamrocks, how was I ever going to see him again. Should I take the bike without dad knowing and just go see him, I didn't like to lie to him but what could I do? After a while I could hear dad going back into his bedroom and the TV coming on. I had to think quickly and without too much hesitation I jumped up and got dressed, I needed the toilet so I tiptoed towards it, I tried to be as quiet as I could but forgot and flushed the toilet 'flippin hell' I thought, when I opened the bathroom door my dad was standing there in his dressing gown with a little smile on his face.

"We need to talk" he wasn't going to let things go I thought.

"OK, the talk" I replied as I made my way over to the sofa and sat with my arms hugging my knees.

"I got a fright yesterday, I'm sorry for shouting but I was so worried about you pet, I thought I had lost you for ever" he sat beside me and put his arms around me "you are the most important person, the most important thing in my life, and I never want to let you go".

I felt extremely sad, I didn't want to lose my dad, but I didn't want to lose Shamrocks either.

"Now tell me, where do you be off to every time you go cycling?" He ask concerned. My eyes started to fill with tears "Is it a boy?" he asked looking very upset, I shook my head as the tears started to roll down my cheeks again and I suddenly developed a cold as my nose began to run.

"Then what is it? you can tell me anything" he was over concerned and I had to tell him the truth, I had no other back up plan or lies, I had to tell him and hoped he wouldn't go crazy with me.

"I go visit a horse every day". I said quietly and watched his face for a reaction.

"A HORSE?" He said loudly. I just nodded and said nothing else. "What horse, with who?"

"Nobody, just me" He looked away thinking about it and smiled.

"Whose horse is he and where is it?" He wanted to know more.

"Tommy Walsh's horse, the most fabulous beautiful grey you could imagine" I said hoping he wasn't about to go nuts.

"Not that mad grey horse I hope? The one Kerry knew about?" he said puzzled. I couldn't answer so just bit my bottom lip and nodded.

"Jesus Molly, what are you playing at? That horse is wild, Tommy Walsh is a very respectable trainer and if he thought that horse was unsafe and put him in a field to end his days, then I'm not happy about my baby girl going near him!" He was clearly very upset now and he had stood up and was pacing the floor.

"He's NOT mad" I shouted "He's wonderful, pleeeeease just come and see him with me, nobody is around and I'll show you". I really wanted to show him how wonderful Shamrocks was but he was waving his hands in the air shaking his head.

"NO NO NO WAY" he shouted. "That horse nearly killed one of Walsh's best lads, he ended up in hospital with broken bones and had concussion, you think I want to see you like that?"

He had no idea about this horse, I knew this horse better than anybody and I wasn't going to take this anymore.

"It's not true, Shamrocks is beautiful and I love him" I was crying really hard and I was so upset, I thought my dad was more considerate than this, why was he being so stubborn and why would he believe strangers over his own daughter. Dad was rubbing his hair walking around and breathing heavily.

"Right then, there's only one thing to do" he said sharply.

"What's that?" I asked still crying.

"Show me the horse" he said as he pointed towards the door for us to leave, I jumped off the sofa so quickly and ran to pull on my wellies.

"Ehh dad, maybe you should get dressed first" I said to him as he was picking up his keys for the jeep.

"Oh right, right, give me two minutes" he said as he threw the keys towards me to go start up. I ran downstairs and out the back and unlocked the jeep, I sat in the driver side and started the engine and turned on the heat so he wouldn't be complaining about it being too cold.

When he got into the jeep he joked by going to turn left "DAD" I shouted and pointed to the right.

"I'm only joking..." he said and drove off out of town. I felt anxious and excited but a little terrified, what if Shamrocks doesn't like my dad and goes crazy? That'll be the end of it I thought. We drove for a few minutes and then he asked "Where about is this horse then?"

"A little further" I said.

"This is some cycle you're doing every day, and now I know why you wear the wellies, I thought it must be a silly fashion going around" dad said as he peered out the window left and right, what was he looking for? some mad stallion I thought.

"Just go up this hill and park at the top" I said, as I looked across the fields and there he was, watching the jeep. I wondered if he knew I was in the jeep, did he know what a jeep was, maybe he thought cars were a species of their own.

We got to the top and I jumped out, my dad was looking around eyeing the grey horse.

"Come on" I said as I jumped over the stone wall and landed in my usual spot with a thud "you want to meet him right?" I didn't wait for an answer I just walked on down the field towards Shamrocks "Mornin lads" I shouted to the donkeys. My dad had jumped over and was following me down the hill towards the field with Shamrocks in. Shamrocks didn't look too bothered by my new companion, he stretched his long neck and lifted his head up into the air and gave a long whinney at me. "Shamrocks" I shouted at the top of my voice and with that he galloped with full speed towards the stone wall, I started to run as fast as I could, dad was shouted "Wait" and "Molly watch out" but I knew I was perfectly safe so I ran at full speed. Shamrocks came to a halt his side of the wall and I came to halt my side. I felt like I was in love even though I had no idea what that would feel like.

I climbed up onto the stone wall and Shamrocks turned his body for me to get on his back.

"MOLLY, WHAT ARE YOU DOING?"

Dad was trying to run as fast as he could to stop me mounting Shamrocks, but I totally ignored him, I had to do this to show him he was wrong. So as soon as I mounted him, I felt more confident than I had yesterday and gave him a little kick with my heels on his belly. Shamrocks immediately broke into a canter, ohhh no I thought, I've not done this yet so I sat up straight and kept my balance and moved with the rhythm he was making, one two three, one two three, one two three... this was far more comfy than the trot was, I used my legs like I did yesterday to turn and steer him and he went left, right, straight and then in a straight line I would shift my legs back a little on the right and I could feel him do a little hop, then back a little on my left and feel him do a little hop. Then as if some powerful strength came over me, I could see the stone wall where my dad was standing in complete disbelief, I got Shamrocks into a nice rhythm for his canter and aimed at the wall.

"NOOOOOOOO" I could hear my dad scream as he tried to get in front of Shamrocks as we approached the wall. as I got closer I could instantly judge my stride and I used my seat even more and pushed one, two, three strides and with that he lifted his front legs raising me high into the air, I had to put my hands on his neck for balance and I leaned backwards as we landed pulling some main out of his gorgeous grey mane.

"WHHOOOOOOWWWWEEEEEEE" I screamed, I could not believe I had just done that!!! I slowed him down and turned him towards my dad and let him relax back into a walk, as we got closer my dad had his hands glued to his head pulling on his hair, he had white knuckles and his face was bright red.

"Holy Mary, Molly, what are you playing at? GET DOWN" he said crossly. I slid off Shamrocks back and stood next to him hugging his neck. My dad walked forward and looked at the horse in the eye, he stretched out and grabbed my arm and pulled me away.

"Why?" I screamed "What's wrong?"

"Get away from that horse" he said sternly and made me stand away from him. He walked over and tried to touch the Shamrocks nose, with that Shamrocks gave a squeal and turned and galloped away.

"You've frightened him" I shouted. I tried running towards him but my dad grabbed me putting both his arms around my body, I started to kick and scream but he wouldn't let me go. I struggled as much as I could, my arms were hurting me and I collapsed on the ground crying.

"You're not to see that horse again, do you hear me?" He said crossly. I didn't answer him I lay in the mud crying and crying. He turned to walk back up the hill, I was so upset, why was he being like this? I proved him wrong, why wouldn't he let me do the one thing I loved?

"MUM WOULDN'T HAVE STOPPED ME" I screamed after him, he just turned and looked sorrowful at me and walked back towards me.

"If your mum was here now, and saw me let you ride the most dangerous, vicious, wildest animal on this planet, she would have me hung dry!" he was emotional too and very upset.

"She would let me, she would" I cried "It was mum who led me to him"

"What?" he said confused.

"He's the only one who knows how I feel and I'm never going to give up on him because he never gave up on me" I cried. I tried to make sense but I wasn't sure if I was. Dad stood scratching his head.

"Get in the jeep" he said and pointed up the hill.

"I don't want to" I said still crying.

"One last time, Molly O'Neil, get in that jeep... NOW!" he raised his voice and it was the first time I felt scared and I did exactly what he said, Shamrocks was stood still the other end watching everything that was going on. I sulkily went up the field and sat in the jeep silently. Dad jumped in the other side and was rubbing his head and sighing

"Right then" he said starting his engine. "Do you really want to ride that lunatic?"

I looked at him excitedly; of course I bloody did "YES YES" I said looking at him with as much hope as I possibly could.

"Well if you're going to ride, then it's not going to be like flipping 'Clint Eastwood', you will need training" he said, but I couldn't let him finish….

"Yes, ohh thank you" I leaned over to kiss and hug him.

"Hang on let me finish.... You need proper training and we'll need to see Tommy Walsh, and I don't know how he'll feel about you and this horse, but we'll try, ok?" he asked as I leaned forward and gave him the most meaningful hug I had ever giving him.

"Thank you sooo much dad, I promise I'll never lie to you again" I exclaimed.

He started the engine and drove on forward and didn't turn around for home as I expected.

"Where are we going to now?" I asked him.

"To see Tommy Walsh" he said.

I looked out the window and watched Shamrock until he was out of sight *'thanks mum'* I was thinking from my heart.

Chapter 6

It was 08.34 am and we approached an entrance with huge iron gates on large pillars with horse's heads on top. Dad rolled down his window and buzzed an intercom. He waited for a few seconds then did it again, and then we heard a voice say "Who is it?" It was a ladies voice and she sounded a little abrupt.

"How are you Mrs Walsh? It's Martin O'Neil here, from O'Neil's pub in Clada" dad said shouting to overcome the noise of the jeep.

"What do you want?" said the woman, dad gave me look and raised his eyebrows to heaven, I laughed and was waiting to hear more from this unhappy woman and actually had butterflies in my tummy.

"I want to talk to Tommy if he's around, about a horse" explained dad.

"Right, right well I suppose you better come in then" and with that she buzzed the large iron gates open.

As we drove up the sweeping driveway I was

astonished by the beauty, never before in my life had I seen or been in anywhere so amazing. The perfect tarmac avenue was sweeping with poplar trees and stud rail fencing enclosed mares with foals frolicking in the paddocks. A huge yellow stately house over looked the land and to the left was a courtyard of stables. The stables were all white with tiled black roof and all had black doors with the top half opened and each housed horses looking out, ears pricked to see who was arriving. Some had blades of hay in their mouth and munched while they looked on. There were people all wearing maroon sweatshirts with TW in white on the back. They were wheeling wheel barrows, leading horses, grooming, tacking up. I was fascinated by the busy yard and the work that was being carried out. As we got out of the jeep my dad said to me "Don't speak, let me do all the talking and whatever you do don't stare!" Stare at what? I couldn't help looking at what was going on, I felt like I was suddenly where I belonged.

A short fat woman came waddling over towards us, she had short wispy grey hair that escaped through a golden coloured head scarf. She had a lazy eye and a scar across her mouth. Her hands were in the pockets of her tweed jacket. She approached us and just gave a nod, no smile. "What can I do for you

Mr O'Neil?"

"Hello mam, how are ye?" My dad put his hand out to shake hers but she kept hers inside her pocket. She didn't reply, I felt embarrassed and she was extremely rude, she just glanced at me and said nothing and turned back to my dad. "Is himself about?"

"He is" she kind of got the hint my dad wanted to see Tommy, not her. "He's behind that row of stables over there, in the outdoor school, training our Jessica" she pointed towards the direction we needed to go. "We have high hopes for our Jessica you know" she bragged.

"Thanks Mrs" said dad as he put a hand on my shoulder and we walked in the direction of the outdoor school, I didn't know what that meant so I asked dad.

"What's an outdoor school? Is this a school for kids and they sit outside?" I felt confused. Dad laughed and explained it was another word for an arena, an arena was where people rode horses and ponies, trained, show jumped, dressage etc... "Ohhh" I replied and as we walked through the yard some of the other people working said hello, some looked stuck up and continued on with what they were doing, all I was interested in was the horses, they all looked so shiny and muscular. Poor Shamrocks would sure love it here I thought.

As we walked behind the stables I saw a huge sand arena, it was full of colourful jumps, poles, stands, a big red brick wall. There was even what looked like a mini swimming pool with some flowers either side. As we stood to watch I could see a girl on a big black horse, she was approaching a set of jumps that looked taller than I was, she rode towards it with her long black hair up in a high pony tail, the horse looked so elegant and so athletic, it took off like an airplane and cleared the jump slowly and softly and landed safely the other side, the girl cantered towards where we stood and just looked at us, she was chewing gum and as she passed us, some sand kicked into our faces. It made me blink and I had to wipe the salty sand from my lips and face.

"That's enough" said a voice from a man who walked from behind the big red wall. He looked as if he was around 60 years old, he had grey hair and a pot belly. He looked over and gave us a wave "Martin how are ye?" he shouted out loud.

"Well Tommy, how's she cuttin?" shouted dad back. The girl had cantered around the arena and now jumped over another jump that had two parts to it, she cleared them fabulously.

"I said that's enough!" shouted Tommy at the girl. Either she can't hear him or she's a little bitch I thought, as she turned towards the massive red brick wall, I could see her trying to place her horse and push for the final strides, but her horse must have thought no way ho-zay and he put his breaks on as she and him slid into the butt of the jump. She didn't hit the ground but with that she raised her whip and gave three hard lashes behind the saddle, her horses ears went back as hard as they could, he stretched his neck and showed his teeth and gums as he tried to get away from her. She yanked at the reins and pulled him to a halt, I could see red drip from his mouth, she must have cut him.

"For fecks sake Jessica" roared Tommy "I said that was enough, now go walk him around and make sure he doesn't stiffen up."

The girl sulkily walked the horse around, she looked curiously over at my dad and I to see why we were there.

"Sorry about that Martin, she's on a new guy we got in from America, and I don't want to over face him, but Jess gets so carried away" he was shaking my dad's hand and he looked at me "So who's this then?"

"This is Molly, my daughter" said dad

proudly.

"I didn't know you had a daughter" he said squinting his eyes in the morning sunshine.

"Yeah, she errr lived in Dublin with her mother but errrr, she passed away in January so now she's stuck with me" Dad gave me a reassuring hug so I wouldn't get upset.

"Ahh Janey Mac, I'm sorry to hear about that, well you're a lucky girl to have such a grand father here" he gave me a little pat on my head as if I was a puppy. "So Martin what can I do for ya?"

"Well, its Molly here, I was wondering if she could get some proper riding lessons from you and see what you make of her?" asked dad.

"Well to be honest Martin, I don't run a riding school, it's a show jumping business I have here, horses here cost hundreds of thousands and I can't afford a novice rider on them" he said as he looked a little baffled why we had come to him "Why don't you try Quinns? They've a nice little yard she could get started at."

"You see the thing is, Molly here has a bit of a gift I think, and I reckon with correct training she could be something". Dad spoke proudly and my heart began beating faster, I was in shock that he thought so highly of me, it was only my second time to sit on a horse that morning, maybe he's getting a little too much carried away I thought.

"Look, we all think our little girls are going to be something of a superstar someday, look at our Jessica, she's 16 now and I've been coaching her since she was in nappies, with a bit of luck with this new horse from America, we may have a shot at the London Olympics next year, so you see, I don't have the time for someone like Molly, I'm very sorry" what he really was trying to say nicely, is that I must be crap and his Jessica is brilliant.

"I understand, I understand. Well thank you for your time anyhow" My dad shook his hand and we were about to leave when he turned and said "You know that old grey that's rotting away in the field on Murphy's Hill?"

"That bastard" said Tommy, "What about him? What's he done now?"

"Will you sell him to me?" Did I hear correctly, what the hell was going on, I kept my mouth shut like dad said and my ears extra open.....

"Sell him? Why? Are you going to send him to France for me?" said Tommy laughing at his own joke.

"Well, I have a Shetland out the back of the pub and he needs a friend, saw your guy looking lonely and thought maybe they could both keep each other company". What was he on about I thought, what Shetland?? Dad gave me a sharp look, I didn't dare speak!

"Well, he's a bit mad, nobody here can ride him, if you want him, you can have him... for free, but don't come back here complaining if he's bit someone or worse". Was he serious? I couldn't believe this!

"How much do you want for him?" asked dad very much down to business now.

"He's your for nottin" said Tommy

"I'd like to buy him all the same, so we know where we stand. How much?" said dad sternly. Tommy thought about it for a moment then what I heard next I could not believe.

"Give me one euro, and I'll give you his passport, and he's yours. I never want to hear any problems about him, he's your responsibility.... deal?" said Tommy.

"Deal" said dad as they both spat on their

hands and then shook, it was the most gross thing I had seen but in my head I was screaming Oh My God Oh My God! I couldn't believe it! Shamrocks was going to be ours! We followed Tommy into the big house, it was full of gleaming trophies and cups in glass cabinets, rosettes filled every wall, Jessica sure was good I thought even though she was rude.

As dad and Tommy spoke about people they knew, they exchanged the one euro coin and he handed my dad the passport for Shamrocks.

"Right Tommy, make sure and call in for a pint sometime, on the house" said dad as we were leaving.

"I sure will, and the best of luck with that grey, just make sure your little one doesn't ride him!" he said a little concerned, but not that concerned I thought. "You're covered in mud child, what happened to you?" he asked looking a little wary.

"I ehhh, I ehhh" I looked at my dad for help who didn't really know how to lie so I finished "I fell of my bike."

This made Tommy laugh as he said "Well, maybe you should get lessons on your bike before you try the four legged creatures" My dad laughed also at his joke, little did Tommy Walsh know it was his pretend laugh.

At that moment Jessica came into the house wearing gleaming long shiny black boots, canary coloured jodhpurs and a black turtle neck, her hair still in a pony tail, she just looked me up and down and walked by me towards another room. Tommy shook his head and said quietly to my dad "teenage girl's ehh? nightmare to keep control of"

"yeah yeah" lied my dad as he looked at me as if to say *'not you pet!'* " Well I'll see you around, take care."

We left the house and got back into the jeep. As we drove down the avenue towards the big gates, my dad passed me the passport with a big smile on his face. I let out the biggest scream of excitement, I couldn't believe it, Shamrocks was mine! All mine!

"OK, now two rules... one, you promise to look after him? And do some shifts on weekends in the bar to help pay for his keep?" I nodded excitedly and was bouncing up and down in the seat "Two, you get proper lessons, and we buy you some tack, and finally... three...." he stopped the car and looked serious at me "never be a stuck up little bitch like that Jessica!" he was delighted for what we just did, I was so happy, I couldn't wait to see Shamrocks and tell him, and take him to his new home.

"Where we going to keep him?" I asked wondering what stables were around us.

"Well, I was thinking we could convert the old barn out the back into a stable, and ask Bill if we could fence off some of his field for a paddock to graze him in and ride" It all sounded too good, I was so excited I jumped over to hug my dad beeping the horn on my way.

"I love you dad" It was the first time I said it out loud and it brought tears to his eyes.

"Who'd have believed that one euro could make someone so happy?" he asked delighted.

"You better believe it dad!"

Chapter 7

We worked all day and into the night, my dad went back and forwards to the timber yard buying wood, hinges, drinkers, everything you could possibly imagine that we may need for a horse. I went to the local news agent and bought Horse and Hound to try found out what things I would need for Shamrocks. I was reading the magazine in between holding timber for my dad as he cut it and holding partitions up while he nailed and hammered them into position. It was dark and I could see people heading into the bar for their evening out. Kerry had popped out a couple of times to check on us, the last time she brought two shepherds pies and two glasses of milk for us to have outside. It was one of the happiest moments of my life, working with my dad was so much fun, it didn't feel like work at all. I was missing mum but knew she would be smiling down on us. I was feeling a little tired when people were leaving the pub and my dad asked what time it was, I looked at my watch, it was 12.44am!

"You go on up to bed pet, I'll finish a bit here and we'll go get him tomorrow" said dad.

"Are you sure, I don't mind staying" I told

him, but I was very tired and feeling a bit cold but hadn't let on to him.

"You go on up and I'll see you in the morning" he said. I gave him a kiss and went inside, Kerry was just finished tiding things up.

"You excited Molly?" she asked me.

"Yeah, I can't wait for Shamrocks to live here" I was still in shock a bit.

"Shamrocks?" she asked "That's a funny name, well you go on to bed I'll bring your dad out a cuppa".

I could hear her humming a song as she made a cup of tea for my dad, does she not have a boyfriend to go home to I thought, she's always here.

I was so tired and didn't realise it until my head hit my pillow, I kissed mums picture before turning out the light and hugging Bobo. Tomorrow my new horse was going to be here, I couldn't wait!.

Next morning I was up, dressed and outside before Bill arrived. "Be jayzes Molly you should be a post woman" he said when he saw me filling up buckets of fresh water and filling a new haynet.

"I've got a new horse Bill" I told him excitedly.

"Ohhh I know, I know. Tell your dad I'll be around tonight to fence off an area for him in the field" he pointed to the where the annoying cows were.

"Cool, thanks Bill" I said.

"So do you have everything you need for him?" he asked.

"I don't really know what I need" I said honestly, "this was all new and I didn't know what saddle, bridle, bit etc... I thought maybe someone might be able to help us".

"Sure your dad will be able to help you with all that" he said "Sure wasn't he on the national pony show jumping team when he was a lad".

"What?" I asked in disbelief.

"Has he not told you? yeah Martin was one cool kid when he was 16, gave it all up when he met your mother, said he needed to get something solid in place if he was to get her and you to live here, but sure you know all this?" he looked worried now, because no, I had no idea about this, the word show jumping and horses have never been mentioned to me before! I left a bucket filling with water and stormed upstairs to my dad's room, he was still asleep but woke and looked at me surprised "What's wrong pet?" he sat up quickly he knew by my face that something was up.

"National Irish Pony Team?" is all I said. And I waited for him to reply.

"Look, I was going to tell you eventually, but I never got a chance, anyway it was a long time ago and sure I was just a kid" he rubbed his sleepily eyes but I wasn't going to let this one go.

"Just a kid, you weren't just a kid to father me at the time" I felt a bit bad inside, but I was upset he never mentioned something like this before.

"Come here, come here. Look if you want to know everything then here it is..." he sat up straighter and took a deep breath. "I had just turned 16 and was selected to jump on the Irish team at the RDS, Dublin. I rode a pony called Mulligan and when I was in Dublin I saw the most beautiful blonde girl who was working in the office taking entries for the show, this was your mum. Her parents were very well off and sure I thought I had no chance, but with a bit of luck at the shows disco I asked her to dance, and well, one thing lead to another.... when her parents found out she was pregnant they kicked her out, my parents sold my pony and told me to grow up and that's how it was. But none of it was a mistake, we both knew as soon as you were born, that you were a gift from God himself". He leaned over to give me a hug, here I was complaining, and all that they had gone through at a young age to have me to bring up, and now here I am with my father who loves me very much and has just got me a horse!

"I'm sorry" I said "I had no idea what you both went through".

"You don't need to know, important thing is now, you're with me, we're a team and your beautiful mother up in heaven is smiling down on us right now". He moved to the edge of the bed "Right, put the kettle on, we have a busy day today, tack to buy, riding clothes for you madam and what else...." he was thinking to himself with a ridiculous look on his face.

"Shamrocks!" I said excited again.

"Ohh yeah, the donkey.... Shamrocks, that's an awful flippin name" I knew he was joking.

"He likes it" I said as I headed towards the kitchen to make him breakfast.

"This is a first by the way!" he called to me, nodding at me making breakfast before he went into the bathroom for a shower.

Dad insisted we were going to do this right. There was only one shop in the whole of Ireland that he would buy my tack and clothing from, Byrnes Saddlers in Sligo. He knew everything I needed to get, show jumping saddle, numnahs, girth, stirrups, bridle, head collar, hat, boots, jodhpurs and at the end he said to the sales lady who must have worked on commission and today was like Christmas for her "Can you fit her for a show shirt and try that black jacket too, the one on sale over there" the lady brought out lots of different styles for me to try on, but the one on the sale fit best, it had a gold lining on the inside, he got me a shirt with a collar and some white jodhpurs too.

"Why do I need these?" I asked him, they were beautiful but I couldn't see myself hacking around Clada in them.

"Ahh you never know, might do the odd gymkhana or something some time" he said.

As we left, the jeep was stuffed with tack, clothes, rugs and a few books for me to read which I immediately got stuck into. The whole way back I kept asking him what things meant like; "What's the frog?" and he replied;

"It's on the sole of the hoof, don't worry about it",

So I did just that. We drove on a little more and then I asked him. "What's the Sheath?"

"That's his willy, again don't worry about it, it'll clean itself no matter what the book says" and then after I asked him another question he said to "put them books away"

"Dad, will you train me?" I looked at him with puppy eyes.

"Ohh no, not puppy eyes! Do you really want me to? Because I can ask Tommy Walsh again if you like?" He suggested.

"And see that Jessica every day? No thanks!" I said shaking my head.

"Right, well first thing we have to do is settle him in, make him feel at home and let him know that we're his friends, that he has more than just you, we're a team now".

"Team O'Neil!" I said "Super Team O'Neil, Dad and daughter Team O'Neil, Molly O'Neil

Team, Martin the Great & Co."

"OK OK I get it, calm down you're too excited!" he said, I knew he was excited too but he was trying to keep a level on it all.

Back home dad reversed the jeep to our new stables. It had one stable and a little tack and feed room beside it, it was perfect and as I jumped out Kerry was standing there smiling with Bill, she moved to the side and there on the door was a beautiful brass plate that read "Shamrock".

"I hope you like it" she said to me, my dad gave her a loving smile and a wink.

"Ohh Kerry I love it, thank you soooo much" I went over to give her a big hug, and found myself giving her a kiss on the cheek, she looked pleased and stroked my hair. I then got all our bits and pieces out of the jeep to give them a new home, it didn't take long. I checked over the bed that had been newly laid for Shamrocks arrival, his water was crystal clear and his new hay net hung beside his door so he could munch and look out at the same time.

"Are we ready to go get him?" asked dad, I

didn't need to answer I jumped into the jeep ready to go.

"Well, what are you going to catch him with?" asked dad.

"What do you mean? Sure I don't need anything" I said.

"Did you forget what I said earlier, from now on, were going to do things the right way, go get a head collar and lead rope" he pointed towards the new tack room, I jumped out and got them quickly looking up one of my new manuals to make sure I was getting the right thing, I had picked a bright green coloured one so it would make Shamrocks look distinguished. I jumped back in beside my dad and couldn't wait to go get him.

When we arrived at the top of the hill he was still loose in the field with the donkeys, he knew the jeep this time *'clever boy'* I thought, as he came galloping over to the wall to greet us. I jumped over and without any hesitation he let me slip the head collar over his head. I had some carrot flavoured horse treats for him that we got from the tack shop earlier, he munched them all real quickly "what a piggy" I said to him, he sure did have a sweet tooth!

I looked around as did my dad for the gate, where was it? There was no way in or out, what a strange field we were saying.

"We'll have to drive all the way around to the far road, it looks like the gates go that way and onto that road over there" he was pointing miles away through fields and fields, this was stupid I thought, I had an idea but I didn't want to upset him, so I just went ahead and vaulted onto his back and kicked him into a canter.

"Molly get down" he shouted, I knew he was mad but I seriously knew I was ok, so I headed for the wall once more and without a shadow of doubt we both cleared it and came to a halt pretty soon after landing the other side, so there was no real need for him to over react I thought. "You pull a stunt like that once more, and he will be going to France, I mean it!"

"Ahh dad, he had a head collar on" I said.

"No hat, no bridle, no saddle, no nottin, starting from now... ok?"

"Ok" I said and headed off down the road towards home.

"Molly, get down and walk" he shouted. I

had to do what he said, so I got off him and led him down the road, he walked swiftly, I think he knew he was coming home with me and he was proud stepping out every stride as if he was walking on the red carpet in Hollywood.

"See ya later dorks" I shouted over to the three donkeys. Once again, they never budged an inch. "OK Shamrocks, let's take you home".

Chapter 8

We had Shamrocks home and my dad was making me work.... work.... work.... He gave me tasks to do each day and said it would all come together like some great plan. I think he was watching the 'A-Team' too much! He showed me how to groom Shamrocks correctly, pick out his feet and put his tack on. Then I would have to practice this several times a day, before school, after school and before I went to bed. He also showed me how to lunge and insisted I do this for at least two weeks. He thought me control of voice and body language, Shamrocks had got used to all of us and loved all the attention he was getting from everyone. I used to take him to the shops down the town, Mrs Hegarty wasn't too pleased when I tied him outside the shop to a bargain basket she had on display, when I came out with a packet of polo mints for him he had a water pistol gun caught in his head collar.

"Get that horse out of my shop" she screamed "You're turning me customers away".

"What customers" I replied, she didn't look too impressed so I put the pistol down out of Shamrocks mouth and pulled him away. "Stop nicking stuff, you'll get us arrested" I tried to tell him. As we walked back towards the pub I noticed some girls from my class coming towards me, Oh no it was Roisin and her two side kicks. They were giggling as they linked each other walking along. I'd seen girls like this in Dublin before, they never interested me, they were always the ones to slag the unfortunate.

"See your walking your oversized dog again O'Neil?" said Roisin in the middle, the other two thought her comment was classic and started to laugh pathetically.

"Takes one to know one" I said and continued on down the road.

"That's Original" she shouted after me "have you nothing better to fight back with?"

I just walked on home towards our pub when I heard her shout "go on back to daddy, daddy's girl" and then she said the most spiteful thing of all "or are you mummy's girl? Oh yeah I forgot, she's dead!"

I stopped in the middle of our quiet village street and turned around, my heart began to ache, she was so horrid. The other two idiots were laughing, Roisin just smiled and turned to walk into Hegarty's shop. What a bitch, I'll show her someday. I felt very upset but who the hell does she think she is? "Come on Shamrocks, let's get out of here" and we headed home.

Several days went by, was I ever going to sit on Shamrocks again? Dad had me mucking out, grooming, tacking up, un-tacking, lunging.... I had to work Saturday nights as a lounge girl in the bar, picking up empty glasses and taking orders, I earned ten euros from dad plus tips, at the end of my first night I had over sixty euros, this aint bad! So I asked could I work Friday's too, Sundays were off limits because of school next day.

I was skipping out Shamrocks (taking the pooh out) a term I learned from my books and dad came around to see me.

"You ok pet?" he asked.

"Yeahhh, just doing stuff" I replied

"Well, I was thinking, it's been a while now and you've been good. You've worked hard and not broken any rules, so how about it then?"

"How about what?" What was I going to

have to do now?

"Tack him up" instructed dad. Ohh dear God, for the millionth time, I got all his stuff and tacked Shamrocks up.

"He thinks you're a My Little Pony!" I told Shamrocks. When I was finished I asked "Now what? un-tack?".

"No...." he said "get your hat".

I looked at him amazed, I didn't say anything and just walked as fast as I could into the tack room, I had my hat and boots all ready for this moment! I put them on as fast as I could wasting no time at all. When I came out dad had already lead Shamrocks into the paddock. He had the caveson and lunge line over the bridle.

"I thought you said get my hat and boots" I said crossly as he began to lunge him.

"I'm just warming him up for a few minutes" he lunged Shamrocks on the left rein then on the right rein, walk, trot, canter, halt. He was looking a lot more muscular now than when we first took him home. My dad approached him and looked at him all over.

"What we'll be working on is you getting a

correct seat, and turning this muscle here" pointing to the top line of Shamrocks neck "all built up like Sylvester Stallone!" I didn't understand but just agreed to anything, I just wanted to sit on Shamrocks again!

"Now young lady, no more fancy vaulting and definitely, no more bareback.... put your left foot in this stirrup here and gather your reins in your left hand... ok?"

"Yep" I eagerly gathered the reins and did what he said, I pulled myself up with ease and before my bottom hit the saddle I had my other foot correctly in the opposite stirrup.

"Now put your right foot in the right stirrup" he said instructing, as he walked around and found I had it already done, "good, good" he didn't take the lunge line off, I thought he was going to set me free and let me gallop off into the sunset. "Right, walk on nice and azey and do as I tell you, no ifs or buts, do you understand?" I dare not disagree so I just nodded and squeezed Shamrocks into a walk on the left rein, my dad corrected my whole posture, he made me sit taller, keep my heels down, keep my hands up, keep my thumbs on top, shoulders back, he put the yard brush between my elbows behind my back to make me sit tall and correct, it hurt every time I moved wrongly.... he went through everything and kept repeating it all the time. As soon as I thought I had it all right he would yell something else, then back to what I thought was right. We walked and walked for about an hour, I was bored and starting to feel really sore.

"Can we not go any faster?" I asked.

"He who must walk must learn to creep.... you must learn to walk before you trot!" he said. Kerry had arrived and was standing to the side watching on.

"Come on Molly show me your stuff" she giggled and got a scornful look from my dad, "Awe come on Martin give her a break." but I didn't want a break, I wanted to know more. My dad pulled me into the center and patted Shamrocks.

"You can hop down now" he said sternly. I jumped off not impressed, I was waiting for weeks to sit on him and all we did was walk! "Come here" he said grabbing my arm and lifting my sulky head "Good things come to those who wait".

"I'll go un-tack him, come on Shamrocks before you fall over with boredom!" and I led him back to his stable.

Next day, same thing. Walk, fix my heels, legs position not right, sit up taller, my thumbs were not on top of my reins, heels down again, shorten my reins, shoulders back, yard brush again... this went on for 9 days, I was clearly bored and Shamrocks ears waved backwards more than forwards and he swished his tail and gave the odd sigh. We were so bored that I closed my eyes while riding to make the movement more thrilling, and when I opened them my dad had been walking directly in front of me, he laughed to my astonishment.

"Right..... Let's do it trot this time" he said slowly.

"Oh my God" I said out loudly, I even startled Shamrocks, I pat his neck to reassure him "Did you hear that Shamrocks, we passed our first test, there's nothing stopping us now... trotting here we come!"

"Right enough of the sarcasm thank you very much, now first you'll learn to sit then we rise.... so take away your stirrups and off you go, trot on..."

Thank goodness I thought. Trotting at last! It wasn't easy to sit to his stride but at least it was more challenging than the walk, again my dad repeated every last detail he said in walk to me, it was so hard to keep thinking about everything he was telling me and concentrate on what I was to do. We worked on our trot for several days and getting the transitions from trot to walk and walk to trot, then I learned how to do extended trot, this was class.... "wwwoooooooowwwwww" I shouted when Shamrocks floated me along and using my seat I could bring his trot right back really slowly and on again. For a little while my dad hadn't been shouting and telling me what to do, then he said "And canter" I checked to see was I hearing things?

"What?"

"Canter!" he replied.

I sat quietly and pushed with my seat for that extra touch and smoothly and softly we were cantering, it wasn't the helter skelter canter that we had in the field, this felt controlled, relaxed and distinguished. Again I got the odd instruction to keep my shoulders back but all in all I could sit silently and move with Shamrocks movements effortlessly.

"Ok, come back to a walk and come here..." dad then rolled the lunge line as we got closer, he went over to Shamrocks head and undid the cavason head collar, took away the sweeping brush and gave me back my stirrups. "Ok you two, show me what you got!" I shortened my reins and squeezed Shamrocks forward to a walk, making sure my pace was not too fast or too slow, then I silently squeezed him to a trot and we went all the way around the outskirts of the paddock we had sectioned off, I changed the rein which means change the direction in which we were going and pushed for a long extended trot across the arena, he extended so much I could see a quick flicker of his hoof over his head between his ears. Shamrocks responded magnificently to my aids, and then I pushed into a canter. A nice easy rhythm to start and then I sat quietly and signaled for him to extend, then back to a short slow canter again, never breaking into a trot he bounced easily as I turned towards the center line and signaled with my right leg behind the girth keeping my left leg on the girth and he did a little hop and changed his lead to the left, then I did the opposite two strides later and he changed to the right, I did this about six times and when I was at the other end I cantered to the corner, and across the arena again, doing the same only not every two strides, but every stride. This was so much fun, I could do this all day for the rest of my life and never get down.

"Ok, come here that's enough" said dad

walking into the center of the paddock. Kerry was watching from the side, I looked over to see her, Bill and Mick all standing watching me along with a few people from the bar, some still holding their pints of Guinness, they all stood watching in silence. 'Ohh no, am I that rubbish?' I thought 'probably doing it all wrong'.

"Hi" I waved over at the gathering crowd. Kerry's mouth was open and she just put her hand up to wave blankly at me.

My dad looked at me, he was sweating and started to stammer a little which I never heard him do before... "Where did you learn that?"

"Why, what have I done wrong?" I was worried that he was going to say 'get down and don't ever sit on this horse again!

"Jesus Mary and Joseph" I turned to see who said that, I couldn't believe it, it was Mrs Hegarty from the shop down the road, what the hell was she doing here?, in fact when I looked around practically the whole village had been watching us.

"Dad" I said, I was nervous and worried "What's wrong?" I felt like I should cry but then my dad turned to the crowd...

"Did you all see that or am I dreaming?" he beamed up at me "Molly, you're a natural! As God as my witness, what you just did there.... people who have ridden all their life can't even accomplish such a thing, do you even know what you did?"

"No.... bunny hop things, Shamrocks likes to canter and do bunny hops" I was giving him a pat as I talked.

"Bunny hop..." he laughed out loud "they're called 'flying changes', the most precise flat work movement you can do, and you did them perfectly, never missing one beat, you even did one time changes!" He was patting Shamrocks on the side of his neck; I thought he might hurt him, he patted him so hard.

"Well, all I know is that we both like doing bunny hops, can I cool him off now and get him ready for bed?"

"Course you can" he said and he headed towards the crowd. I could hear them talking and saying how good I was and how lovely Shamrocks was, I heard Mrs Hegarty say before she left "tell her to pop in with him next time there out for a walk"... she's changed her tune I thought.

That night when I went upstairs to see what was for tea, my dad had a couple of videos for me to watch, he had to go downstairs to the bar but said he would be up soon, I sat in front of the TV with my spaghetti bolognese he had made for me and turned on the video. The first one started with music that was from Star Wars then in yellow writing on a black background said "Martin O'Neil, 148cm Grand Prix Dublin riding Mulligan" and then it showed a boy riding a grey pony cantering towards the first jump, up and over... and this went on the whole way round... this was my dad I thought! I put in the second video, this was form Millstreet International Co.Cork, again it was him this time it even showed the presentation and he got a huge cup and rosettes, then form Cavan, Galway and even South View in England, my dad was a hero when he was 16! As I finished them all and looked over one or two more I was so proud of my dad, he looked so professional, why doesn't he still ride? Maybe I can get him on Shamrocks some time.

After a few hours my dad came upstairs. "Well, did you have a look?"

"Dad! You were so cool, and your pony looks just like Shamrocks!"

"Well, it was a long time ago..... And I err

was thinking, if you wanted, maybe tomorrow we could see how he goes over a few little jumps?"

"If I wanted? are you kidding me? Of course I do, only don't invite the village this time!" I said seriously, it was a bit weird why they all gathered to watch.

"Will do my best, but I can't help it if your building up a bit of a fan club".

With that I was so tired and my bottom ached from so much riding today. "I think I'll go to bed" and I gave my dad a kiss and went to the door to go downstairs.

"Where you off to?" he asked.

"To kiss Shamrocks good night" I took an apple and headed out into the night to give him his nightly kiss and hug. When I approached him he gave a soft whinny. I gave him a huge hug and whispered 'tomorrow we get to jump.... so go to sleep and don't be talking to them cows in the field'. As if understanding what I said he whinnied again softly as I waved good night. I couldn't wait until tomorrow.

Chapter 9

I felt sick. I didn't know what to do! We had prepared, prepared, prepared, but nothing had prepared me for this. I had watched maybe ten riders go and I knew my dad had said when sixteen had gone I was to meet him in the practice arena. I ran to the nearest toilet, there was a long queue, oh no and to make matters worse there was only one toilet and everyone was silent and you could hear every trickle, every flush.... I needed to find someplace else.

I walked around the back of some horse trucks until I found an isolated area and then I put two fingers down my throat, it didn't take much encouragement for my cornflakes to come back up. I felt like I needed to get sick more but then the commentator made an announcement;

"And next into the arena is number sixteen, Jessica Walsh riding Mr Big, and good luck to you Jessica....." then the bell rang. Oh God, number sixteen, dad will be looking for me everywhere. I spat out the remaining gunk and wiped my mouth with the sleeve of my black show jacket. "Oh Pickles!" I said looking down I could see spots of sick on my new black show jacket, I pulled some grass from the verge near where I was and rubbed it. Then I heard a loud cheer from the arena and the posh commentator that sounded like he was from England say "Oh yes, that's the way to do it.... A lovely clear round from Jessica Walsh and it's the only clear we have so far, well done Jessica, next to go is number seventeen......"

I ran as fast as I could to the practice arena, my dad was walking Shamrocks around. Shamrocks looked so smart, he had perfect plaits along his main, he had a new white saddle cloth under his saddle, his hooves shined and he looked spick and span from all the grooming he gets.

"Molly, were the hell where you? There's only three in front of you now, come on let's get a move on..." he gave me a leg up onto my gleaming shiny saddle as I quickly gathered my reins and squeezed Shamrocks straight into a canter. I had strict instructions to do no fancy work, just practical warm up and a pop over a couple of fences, I changed the rein a couple of times doing our little bunny hops in the middle. A few onlookers were admiring us but I was concentrating on what I needed to do and had my ears open to listen to everything dad had to say.

"Right Molly, nice and steady pop over this cross pole" said dad, I cantered around and sailed over the X shaped jump, Shamrocks got a little excited so I had to sit quiet and not encourage him to take advantage. I could see dad putting the jump up straight and again we popped over it, he put it up about four cup holes on either side of the wings, it was no trouble to Shamrocks to just sail over them, he loved jumping, he was so easy to place and he always just picked up and carried me safely to the other side. Then after a couple of jumps I heard the steward in the pocket shouting from his loud speakerphone "Molly O'Neil to the pocket now, you're next"

'Ohhhh mammy mammy mammy' I said quietly to myself, I felt extremely sick again, I could feel it rising up my throat but I tried to think about my course and ignore it, thankfully kindly it went down again.

"Are you ok?" asked dad, he was standing next to me at the pocket which is the term used for the entrance to the arena. "You look white as a ghost, do you want to leave it pet?"

"No bloody way, I haven't got blisters on my backside to back out now" I said crossly.

"That's my girl... now, do you know your

course?" he questioned me as I went over the course in my head I knew it inside out. "And remember after the double sit quietly and put in four strides to that upright, not three like it walks, he's only a little chap" he patted Shamrocks hard on his neck, I wish he wouldn't do that, it might hurt him.

I had noticed that some of the other riders all entered the arena cantering in, they would halt and sometimes go over the course with their index finger, some gave a courtesy nod or bowed to the judge and then when the bell would ring they started the round. I didn't think about this, I was feeling so sick it was the last thing on my mind, the steward opened the rope for me to enter in to the arena and my dad said "good luck pet, do your best no matter what".

I walked into the arena in a slow pace, it felt strange. I felt alone, even though there were faces all around the edge watching, it was the loneliest place I had been for a long time. I've got Shamrocks I thought, I'm not alone. The commentator announced me into the arena and then I heard the bell ring for us to start our round. I knew I had one minute to go through the start. I hadn't decided if I should bow, salute, go over the course.... I was so nervous, my heart was beating so fast and I felt like throwing up again. I looked over at my dad and he looked at me seriously and just gave me a nod. I looked at the judge, he had glasses and was smoking a pipe, he also gave me a long nod. Instead of bowing back to him, I don't know why, but I blessed myself. I felt a lump in my throat because I suddenly thought about mum. I better get going or I'll get eliminated for not starting within one minute. The first jump was a rustic parallel, it looked inviting enough but I was feeling so sick I found it hard to concentrate and the feeling in my legs suddenly turned to jelly, what was happening to me?

    Shamrocks just carried me over the first jump, I felt relieved to have cleared the first, I looked for the second which was a brightly coloured upright, again, I sat quietly and my little hero below me was taking me safely over the next jump and the next and the next… I was feeling more and more sick as the course went on. I was loving the control, the challenge but I couldn't help the way my tummy was feeling. I did exactly as my dad had instructed after the double and sat for four strides, Shamrocks popped popped popped and sailed over every jump with no hesitation, he never touched a pole, and as we landed over the last jump I could see the finish flags. I was so delighted it was over, so relieved, so much so that I relaxed too much and forgot the control I was having over my throat and as I flew through the finish I felt lumps rushing up my neck and filling my mouth, I couldn't hold it in, there was nowhere else for it to go but out... like a spraying hose pipe my sick embarrassingly went all over poor Shamrocks beautiful plaited mane and all down my jacket and onto my jodhpurs, because I was riding against the wind I heard a groan of "ohhhhhh" and I closed my eyes thinking please God no....... but when I looked over to the crowd some of my sick had hit the face of a pretty girl with brown hair in a tight bun, she was wearing an emerald green riding jacket with the Irish flag on the top left corner. Oh no, I realised who she was! It was Jessica Walsh whom we bought Shamrocks from. I brought Shamrocks back to a walk and looked for my dad to exit the arena as quick as I could, some people were laughing and pointing, I felt humiliated and wanted to just kick Shamrocks into a full steam gallop and get out of there forever. My dad had a handful of grass to give to Shamrocks and he patted him really hard as he said "Well done pet, that was amazing, you did so well... what's the matter?" he asked as he saw my eyes fill with tears as I tried not to look at anyone around me for I knew they were all staring and laughing at me. I couldn't answer him, I was so embarrassed and then I heard a posh voice behind me shout.

"Oi, you on that grey! What the hell do you think you're playing at?" I looked at the girl who was standing behind me, she was covered in my sick.... oh dear God what do I say? "I have a jump off to do, and look at me, I'm ruined, do you know how much this jacket cost and now it has your bloody puke all over it!"

"I'm really sorry" I said honestly, "I couldn't help it" I wanted to gallop away but dad held onto my reins and I couldn't go anywhere.

"Oh you will be sorry! That grey, he's the mad horse we sold to you is that right?" she asked.

"What about it?" asked dad stepping in.

"Well that horse is a nut! So you're obviously giving him something to have him so calm and jumping the way he is" she said at the top of her voice.

"Hold on now missy, are you accusing us of doping our horse?" dad was clearly getting angry with her.

"I'm just stating what everyone here is talking about" she walked up closely and looked me in the eye "well at least it'll be as far as you will ever go, in this game you need guts... and not the type that fly out your mouth" she walked away and tore off her jacket shaking her head in discuss "see you in the jump off.... new girl!"

"You watch your mouth young lady, I'll be having words with your father about this!" dad said to her as she was leaving. With that she turned around and stuck up two fingers at us both. "The little bitch!" he said to me under his breath. "Now listen to me you, why are you upset?"

"Because I got sick!" I said slowly. I felt humiliated.

"Well get yourself together, you have a jump off to do and the only way you can get back at that little cow, is show her what your made of...." he made me feel a bit better by adding "not puke!"

I dismounted and ran to the toilets to freshen up, a woman who was in the queue congratulated me on such an effortless round, and also another young girl said she loved my grey and asked what his name was. When I came out dad was walking Shamrocks around keeping him warm.

"Now, we've not planned this part...not that I didn't think you would go clear and make it to the jump off... I just thought we might have a go, see how well you did and we would take it from there" he was scratching his head trying to explain. "So anyhow, here's the thing.... a jump off is when the course is shortened..."

"Good" I interrupted.

"... as I was saying, the course is shortened, but against the clock."

"What clock?" I looked around to see was there some giant clock we were going to chase?

"It means, the timer will start when you go through the beams at the start, you do your course and the time finishes when you go through the finish beam.... do you understand?"

"No, not really" I said honestly.

"Never mind, no time to explain again, here's the course....." and dad went over the course with me. It wasn't jump numbers 1,2,3 and so on.... it was stupid I thought, the course builder had designed the jump off to be 1, 5, 7, 4a 4b and finish over no.3. It looked twisty and tourney and I had no idea what to do. Dad went over the course showing me what tight turns to take and how to approach them, it was a lot harder than the first round, I kept going over the numbers in my head, every time getting it wrong! There were five riders clear in the first round, this meant that me and Shamrocks were sure to be placed fifth at least, I was now excited at the fact we would be going home with a rosette to hang in the tack room. I gave Shamrocks a polo mint to celebrate and dad shouted at me for doing so, "he could get sick if you feed him between rounds!"

I was last to go in the jump off, I watched the first one go. It was a guy on a big bay horse, he knocked both parts of the double but had a good time, I started to warm up Shamrocks again but I heard from the commentator that the next person in also had some faults. The third person went clear but there time was slower, but that put them into first place. As I was finished we went over to stand in the pocket and watch the fourth person go just before it was our turn. It was Jessica Walsh, now wearing a pretty navy pinstripe jacket that replaced the green one that caught my sick earlier!

She started her round like a bullet from a gun, she was quick and her turns were tight, her horse was gorgeous, he was the one we saw her ride the day we got Shamrocks. She finished over the last jump and there was a roar form the crowd as she had gone clear with the fastest time that put her into the lead.

"Ohhh very well done there Jessica" announced the pipe smoking commentator "lovely clear round in a time of 34.05, so that's the time to beat! And can Molly O'Neil, on her debut I do believe... beat that time? she enters the arena now on Shamrocks, the time to beat 34.05" and as I entered the arena dad wished me luck once more.

I passed Jessica as she was coming out "looking a bit green" she said snootily to me. She was such a cow, I wanted to stretch over and just push her off her horse but thought I better not. I walked slowly into the arena again, the bell went and I blessed myself once more. I felt nervous and sick again, at least there was nothing left to throw up so that was an advantage. I squeezed Shamrocks into a canter and instead of flying to the first jump like the others I canter easily and popped over nicely, upon landing I was able to turn him tight to the next jump which we jumped at an angle that nobody else had done, I could hear the crowd say 'aaawwwww'. I kept looking for my next jump and every time I sailed in the air. It was deathly quiet and I could hear the silence of the onlookers. This wasn't as hard as I was thinking, I jumped over the double 4a and 4b then I noticed to the side of the arena still sitting on her horse was Jessica glaring at me.... dam it, I lost my concentration, where was the last jump.... I cantered around and couldn't remember, I looked up at the timer on the clock it was on 23 seconds, 24 seconds... oh no! Now what? I searched all the faces but nobody out there wanted to help, I even saw Jessica again and saw a smirking smile..... then I saw dad he was shouting "THREE" at the top of his voice, then it came back to me, number three, I turned and headed for number three at full speed, there was no checking or thinking about placing him correctly, Shamrocks lifted an sailed higher and wider than ever over the jump, we landed safely the other side and I galloped him through the finish. I looked at the clock and it read 35.42 I smiled widely and went over towards dad, he had a handful of grass for Shamrocks again, patting him hard on his neck and telling me how well we just did.

"That was amazing pet, I'm so proud of you" he was so thrilled we did so well "next time I'll put the satellite navigation on his neck!" we were both laughing when I heard the results being called out "In first place we have Jessica Walsh, second Molly O'Neil..." We both screamed and I bent down to hug my dad. I couldn't believe it, our first show and we came second, I was so chuffed.

We were waiting to go into the arena and I could hear Tommy Walsh talking to his daughter.

He wasn't congratulating her on winning the class instead I heard him say "why didn't you take that first turn after the first jump, I told you it was possible, you never listen!".

"Your never happy are you?" she said and then left to enter the arena to collect her prize. She never looked over at me, but I was so happy to get my rosette, I held it up to show my dad who was waiting for me to come out after our lap of honor which was a gallop around the arena, Shamrocks liked this part, he gave a huge buck as we went around that nearly unseated me. My dad was so thrilled with us, hugging and kissing both me and Shamrocks. As we were heading towards the horsebox Tommy Walsh approached my dad.

"Well Martin, that horse is looking good" he said as he got closer.

"Ahh not too bad now thanks Tommy" said dad as he helped me un-tack.

"Word of advice Martin" he had changed his tune from being friendly to very serious "Don't show up at a show with that horse doped up again, or I'll report you myself!"

"What the hell are you on about?" dad was raging with him.

"That horse is untouchable, not one of our top riders in our yard could even put a head collar on him, and your daughter here, who's only riding a couple of weeks has just come second... nearly winning a major competition.... don't let me have to tell you this again" and just as he turned to walk away my dad grabbed his arm to turn him around.

"Now you listen to me! You can get any God dam test you like done on our horse, the only thing that he's high on is love and talent, pure raw talent that my daughter has. And no matter how many years of training your stuck up little bitch of a daughter gets, she will never compare to what Molly here has. Now feck off and don't you or your daughter ever speak to us again!"

Holy cow! There was no messing with my dad!! Tommy Walsh pushed my dad's arm away in temper and walked away.

"Let's get the flock out of here Molly my love!" said dad. I couldn't wait to get home and tell Kerry all about it, I didn't know what the best part was, coming second and getting a rosette or my dad telling Tommy Walsh to Feck Off!!

Chapter 10

When the summer holidays arrived I couldn't wait to run out of school on the last day as fast as I could. A few others shouted "any plans for the summer?" and "What's the big rush?" but I just ignored them, all I wanted to do was get home to Shamrocks.

It had been hard work, I rode every morning before school for an hour, mucking out and leaving Shamrocks happy for the day until I got home, I then either took him for a quiet hack around the village or just out for a walk, he even walked without a lead rope, he just followed me like a dog. Tom the local Gardá gave me a few warnings "put that animal on a lead" he would shout, but I knew he was only joking. He was a regular in the pub and didn't seem to complain if my dad gave him a free whiskey before heading back to the Garda station on late night duty. Shamrocks and I got to know everyone in the village, a few of the older ladies often stopped and had a carrot in their shopping bag ready to give to him. Dad didn't approve, said he was being spoilt.

When I got home from school I ran over to

Shamrocks, he was in the paddock grazing, I gave him a quick hug and told him the good news that I was home for the summer to take care of him properly. My dad called me into the bar, when I got inside I couldn't focus for a few minutes because the sun had blinded me outside.

"What's up?" I asked as I headed behind the bar to get a coke and packet of cheese and onion crisps. Kerry was there as always she gave me a warm hug and a kiss on my head, she was so loving and I had grown very fond of her.

"Help yourself why don't cha!" said dad, I knew he didn't mind, well at least I thought he didn't! "Post" he said casually and slid an envelope down the bar to me. *Post* I thought *who could this be from?* I was examining the envelope, the post mark said Dublin and SJAI which stood for Show Jumping Association of Ireland. I looked at my dad who just shrugged his shoulders and wanted me to open it and see what it was all about...

I read out loud....

"Dear Molly O'Neil,

We write this letter to invite you to a training assessment day at the RDS, Dublin on the 20th July with your horse Shamrocks. Following your recent success we feel that there may be an opportunity for you to join the International squad and represent Ireland at forthcoming International events."

I couldn't believe what I was reading but dad just said, "READ ON READ ON…"

"The day will involve a full training program with Captain Liam McGowan"

I looked at dad… "Here give it to me…" he said and continued..

" Who you will know from the International circuit, Captain McGowan has requested personally that he would like to meet you and your horse, please confirm that you can attend by calling us on....."

"Ohh my god" I said

Dad read over the letter again word by word as I just did.

"What does this mean?" I asked excitedly with the biggest grin on my face.

"It means, he wants to see how good you two are, and maybe, just maybe, you might get a shot at a major show" dad was so excited he picked me up off the stool and swung me around, he then went over to Kerry and gave her a big kiss on the lips, it lasted a little too long and when they both stopped Kerry just fixed her top and looked at dad scornfully.

"Right Martin, are you actually going to do some work today? I need you to change the barrels, ring the brewery and errr.... we need more nuts" she got her handbag and keys and started heading out the door.

"Where you going?" asked dad, confused by her sudden change in mood.

"I'm going home" she said crossly "I'll be back in a few hours, and you better have those jobs sorted" and with that she had gone.

"What's up with her?" said dad confused.

I gave a big sigh as I was heading out to Shamrocks "Dad, use your head... you'll figure it out!"

"Women!" I could hear him say as I left the bar to go tell Shamrocks the big news.

It wasn't long until the 20th July came around, and we had been working night and day. I was put back on the lunge because according to my dad I was starting to pick up bad habits, so my bottom ached again from no stirrups and having to use my seat to do all the work. And I was jumping with no stirrups or use of my reins. I was nervous that morning, yet relieved because it meant no more intense schooling.... or so I thought!

We had to be in Dublin at 7.30am, this meant we had to leave our house at 04.30 and to load Shamrocks up and be on the road I was up at 03.00, Dad never went to bed at all, as I came down stairs shivering because it was the middle if the night, I caught dad escorting some locals out into the crisp air "safe home now lads, and no going into Galway." They laughed as they left shouting in their drunken state "Ahh you're a gas man Martin O'Neil, God Bless ya".

Dad smacked his hands together and looked jolly as he said "Right, let's hit the road girl!" I slept most of the way despite the cold air blowing in from my dad's window to keep him awake and the Carpenters constantly playing over and over, if I heard *'ohh stop wait a minute Mr Postman'* one more time, I was going to scream!

"We're here, Molly look sharp" said dad as we stopped outside the Dublin School of Equitation. I sleepily pulled myself together as the gates were opened by two soldiers and in the middle of a massive courtyard was a huge statue of a horse, the stables surrounded the yard and grooms in army clothing where flying left and right trying to get as much as they could done as fast as they could. Some soldiers were marching, chanting a song and they all saluted us as they marched by never making any eye contact, I thought it rude not to acknowledge so I saluted back, this amused my dad as he found out where we were to park up. After checking on Shamrocks and giving him a drink we set off to see what was to happen.

  Captain Liam McGowan was a tall man with silver hair, I knew he was one of Irelands greatest riders and had won numerous major championships and even been to the Olympics several times. He looked sternly at us as we walked towards him; he never smiled or looked like he was happy to see us. As we got closer he put his hand out to shake my dad's, he never looked in my direction.

  "Mr O'Neil" he said in a matter of fact tone.

  "Yes it is, hello" said my dad who suddenly seemed like a teenager back stage at a rock concert "It's an honour to meet you sir, I'm a great admirer" The Captain just nodded and then shifted his body swiftly towards me that made me jump a little.

  "So, you must be Miss Molly O'Neil, and

where is this magnificent grey of yours?" he talked down to me I thought.

"He's errrr, errrr, in the horsebox" I replied, I suddenly felt terrified and I knew my dad felt it too but I caught him giving me a wink to reassure me I was ok.

"Well what's he doing in there? Reading the newspaper?" he shouted "go get saddled up and I'll meet you in the sand arena in five minutes". I nodded, turned around and ran as quickly as I could towards the horsebox, good God I only have five minutes to get ready, just then I heard the Captain shout so loud it made me stand still "NO RUNNING IN MY YARD". I was afraid to turn around so I just continued to walk, my heart was pounding so fast and ohhh no... I was feeling sick again like I did at our first show. I was tacking up Shamrocks as fast as I could, poor Shamrocks didn't seem to like being rushed but we had no choice. My dad joined me and told me to get ready and he would finish Shamrocks off. As I mounted and we headed towards the arena, my dad was very silent.

"You scared of the Captain too?" I asked him.

"Bloody petrified!" he said then gave me a grin "Stop worrying, you're making the donkey nervous"

"He's not a donkey" I protested, I hated it when he called him that.

"Look, just do what this man says, he knows everything there is to know about horses, he's a legend and you're honoured to be getting private tuition from him, so just listen, learn and do your best" he gave Shamrocks a massive hard pat on his neck.... agggghhhh, I really wish he wouldn't do that!!!!

I walked around in a circle as the Captain entered the arena and walked up to me, he told me to halt and walked over.

"Heels down" he said. I checked my heels and they were down. Then he said it again "heels down" I said nothing and just looked ahead, then he said on a rather loud tone "heeeels down"

"They are down" I said scared to have answered him at all, ohhh no I've blown it! The one thing I had to do was listen and I just answered him back, he'll make me get down and do fifty pushups.

"OK, lesson number one: never answer me back unless it's something to contribute" he walked around me and Shamrocks, "lesson number two: Do as I say and never argue with what I tell you to do, and finally Molly O'Neil, Lesson number three: I always take two sugars in my tea" he stood in front of me and for the first time smiled. "I'm not as mean as you think, I just need your full attention or we won't be able to work together, understood?" so I slowly smiled and nodded back, weirdo I was thinking, legend or no legend, he seems a bit cuckoo to me.

"OK, off you go and warm him up" he instructed.

After my warm up we began to jump, it was dreadful, we must have been there for three hours. Every time I approached a jump, he yelled something, "Wrong stride, do it again" or "You're being left behind" or "Help the poor chap out" and one I kept hearing over and over and over "Look where you are going, keep your eye on the fence".

I was sweating profusely and Shamrocks neck was like a lather of soap, he looked like a giant advert for fairy liquid. Then at long last he walked into the center of the arena and called me over, he waved to my dad to join us. He kicked the sand around and waited for my dad and gave me the odd look, I was so hot and I could feel my face burning, I ached all over I had never rode for this long on any session before, I thought dad was tough but this guy was in a different league altogether.

"Mr O'Neil, I'll tell you what I think, and this is what I think..." said the Captain, he sure did wriggle his words. "You have a fine horse here, and your jockey has just been truly grilled and she passed the test" he looked at me with a nod. "As you know, I am the Chef De Quip and I am putting together a team, one that I hope I can work with and prepare for future events, so here's what I suggest..." he kicked the sand around some more before finishing "I would like to offer Molly and her horse the chance to travel with the rest of the Irish Team to Italy next week where she can gain some valuable experience and we can take it from there.... so what do you think?"

Dad was grinning like a Cheshire cat, he patted Shamrocks really hard and looked up at me "Did you hear that? The Irish Team!!"

"Seriously?" I said asked, I couldn't believe it. I threw my arms around Shamrocks sweaty neck and gave him a huge hug.

"I take it that's a yes then" said the Captain with a smile "No more jumping until I see you in Italy, I want you both to do light schooling and plenty of pole work.... are you listening?" he asked,

I was so busy hugging and kissing Shamrocks my face was now covered in his sweat, I was only taking in the facts of what he just said,

"Yes, light schooling, poles, we got it" I was beaming so much it made him laugh a little.

"I'll get someone to arrange the details and I will see you in a week Molly. Oh and don't forget your green jacket" he added.

"Oh no dad, I've no green jacket" I knew something like this would cost a lot but dad said not to worry he'd sort something out.

We stopped for lunch on our way home, I was starving, I had never worked as hard as I just did and I ordered a double cheese burger, fries and large coke from the waitress. My dad looked at me and shook his head.

"You're an athlete now young lady, no crap food.... she'll have a Caesar salad and a glass of milk" he told the waitress "and I'll have the burger" he said slyly.

"What?" I asked "Am I fat or something?"

"No, but if you're going to Italy next week, riding in that heat, you need to be fit and trim. Trust me I know" he patted his little pot belly demonstrating.

"Dad" I said honestly "Do you think the Captain likes us?"

"The Captain was a hero when I was riding, I wanted to be him, everyone in Ireland wants to be him, and I can't get over the fact that he thinks my little girl is good enough to jump for the Irish Team" he looked so happy and proud. I just felt happy to make him happy. "And yes, I think he likes us"

"Dad.... can I ask you a huge favour?" I was hoping not to offend him but it was high time I asked.

"Course you can pet, anything" he said concerned.

"Can you stop calling Shamrocks a donkey?" I wasn't joking although he thought I was because he just started to laugh.

"But he is a donkey" he joked.

"And stop smacking him so hard every time you see him, he doesn't like it" I still wasn't joking.

"Tell you what, the day you and Shamrocks get to the Olympics I'll stop smacking him hard and calling him a donkey... deal?" he put his hand out.

"That's so unfair" I said refusing to shake his hand. I sat eating my salad and wondering what the show in Italy would be like, I also was wondering what the juicy burger opposite me tasted like!!

Chapter 11

A sign on our pub said "Gone to Rome around Italy."

"That's stupid" said dad as he read the sign, "who did that?" he asked me and Kerry, who was over the moon when I pleaded to dad to let her come with us. She was my groom I told him, and she had made me the most beautiful emerald green riding jacket with the Irish flag stitched on the top left chest pocket, she even embroidered on my left sleeve in gold thread *'Molly'* and on the right *'shamrocks'*. She also took up a lot of the room with her bags in the back of the jeep.

"And I thought shamrocks was a heavy traveler" said dad looking at the heap of suitcases piled on top of the feed, hay nets, buckets, tack, rugs... the jeep was stuffed and only a small section in the back seat for me as I left Kerry to sit up front with dad. "OK, are we ready?" he asked excitedly, we were all excited, it was a holiday for us all, and Shamrocks was coming too, what more could I ask for. As we drove out the gate and through the town well-wishers filled the street and waved us off shouting *'Good Luck Molly'* and *'Say Hello to the*

Pope' and *'Bring us back a Pizza'* Kerry giggled and waved back to everyone, I caught my dad looking at her with a little smile, I think he was secretly happy I insisted she come along. Was I playing cupid? who knows!

It sure was a long haul.... drive to Dublin and get the boat to Holyhead, then drive to Portsmouth down the south of England to Le Havre, and then through France and into Italy and finally arriving in Rome. It took us four days with stop overs that were pre-arranged for us. There were a few awkward moments when Kerry, me and dad all shared the same bed and once a scream when dad entered into a bathroom when Kerry was having a shower, also at every stop she had to bring in all her bags and took ages to decide on what to wear. It made me think of mum, she was a lot like her, always fashion conscious and never in the same clothes twice.

The drive through Rome was a nightmare, there were people all over the place, they ran in front of cars, they honked their horns, Kerry and dad never stopped arguing over the directions, we were clearly going the wrong way but then we all fell silent as we went deeper into the city and were completely in awe of the beauty that surrounded us. The buildings were so old and magnificent, I pulled out my 'Italy for Idiots' book and pointed out some famous land marks, we had a day trip planned but for now we needed to get to the showground's and Shamrocks to a comfy stable to rest. Our first competition was in two days and tomorrow I was having a one to one with drill sergeant himself!

After several quarrels and wrongly translated instructions we saw a huge sign 'Roma International Horse Show' I sat up as close as I could to the front to see as much as possible, we gave our passes to a man at the gate who in return gave us wristbands to wear and maps that guided us to the stables and around the show grounds. After we finally pulled up and unloaded a stiff Shamrocks I was walking towards stable block 'Pavarotti' number '4511' when I stopped in my tracks. I couldn't believe what I was seeing, for there standing outside stable 4510 was the one and only Jessica Walsh. What the hell was she doing here? She watched me approach with a smug look and as I got closer she slammed her own stable door and walked quickly by Shamrocks and I. What is her problem? And why was she here? Then it occurred to me that I didn't know who else was in the team, I hadn't got to know anyone yet at the shows so I was unfamiliar with who was coming.

Stable 1412 to 1414 also had Irish flags on them, I put Shamrocks into his stable, it had all his details on the door and I was secretly chuffed to see my name beside the Irish Flag saying International Rider. My dad was equally as pleased, and to top it off Kerry insisted we all have photos taken beside the sign. Laughter came from two guys as they walked down the aisle towards us. "Well Martin, save some of that film for the arena" one said.

"How are ye lads?" said my dad pleased to see some friendly faces. One was tall and skinny with blond hair and wore a green polo shirt like the one that was given to me with his name on the back. The other.... when I looked.... was about 5'6" and had sandy blond hair, blue eyes and was without a doubt the best looking boy I had ever seen.

Kerry gave me a wide eyed look as the guys came closer. "Do you know Molly, my daughter? And this is Kerry our groom" dad introduced us.

"Hi Molly I'm Brian" said the tall guy stretching out his hand to shake mine "How are ya Kerry, lovely to meet you".

"Hi" I answered. And I waited for the other fella to do the same, he looked a little shy and then he also shook my hand.

"I've heard a lot about you Molly" he spoke so softly and he sounded like he was from Dublin too "I'm Ted".

"Nice to meet you Ted" I replied. "So who you riding?" I asked looking at the other horses stabled beside Shamrocks.

"Errrr this little mare here" he said showing a bay mare that was next to Shamrocks, he had tried making friends already but she just squealed and nipped him a little before running to the other side of her stable. "She's temperamental" he told me.

I knew I was blushing but I couldn't help it! OK that's enough, I'm here for a reason and meeting boys is not one of them, dad talked a bit about the drive, blaming Kerry for going wrong which in return got a kick from her on his ankles, after I finished settling Shamrocks down and Ted and Brian said their goodbyes, Kerry whispered in my ear "Hubba Bubba!"

"Don't you dare encourage anything like that!" said dad very seriously.

"It's girl talk, stop eaves dropping" she said as she gave him another kick. I liked the way she could boss him around, I needed a few lessons from her.

"Right, Molly you and Kerry, you two go check in to the hotel and I'll sort stuff out here" said dad.

"Are you sure? We can help" I suggested.

"No offence girls, but your both driving me nuts and I've had 96 hours of chitter chatter, so me and Shamrocks need some guy time!" we got the hint, and we were both glad to check into the shows hotel and have a long bath before getting ready for a meal, so we left the boys to it.

I had a bath then fell onto my bed it was after 6.30pm so I thought I could sleep for an hour but instead when I woke it was 11.38pm and no sign of my dad. I was starving too so I pulled on my fluffy pink slippers and headed down the hallway towards Kerry's room. I knocked lightly and listened but couldn't hear anything. They must be in the bar knowing them two there probably grueling some poor bar man over the price of a pint of Guinness and telling him how to pour it right! So I got into the lift and pressed "G" that brought me down to the lobby. It looked quite enough so it didn't matter that I was wearing only my slippers and an oversized green t-shirt with "Shake your Shamrocks" written on it, Kerry had got it for me in duty free on the boat.

"Molly O'Neil" said a soft voice that was walking behind me. It startled me that someone knew who I was and when I turned around I saw Ted who was still wearing his jodhpurs and boots from earlier, team polo and a cap.

"Tim" I exclaimed suddenly feeling very embarrassed and uncomfortable about what I was wearing. Why was I feeling like this? Think of Shamrocks think of Shamrocks....

"You lost? Or are you sleep walking?" his accent was familiar yet a lot more posh than mine.

"Ha, ha, ha" I chuckled that was a good one "I'm looking for my dad or Kerry have you seen them?"

"Yeah, your dad was at the show grounds talking to your donkey, and his girlfriend was there too" he said as he looked around the lobby as if waiting to meet someone.

"He's not a donkey" I actually really did not like it when people referred to him as that. "And you're mistaken, Kerry's not his girlfriend, just our groom friend"

"OK OK don't get all defensive!" he said looking worried that he'd offended me, he put a warm hand on my left shoulder, I could feel my heart beat quicker and I had no idea what to do. Luckily I was saved as I heard a familiar voice enter the lobby.

"What are you doing down here?" asked my dad as he approached us with Kerry behind him. I could see his eyes squinting curiously at us, as Ted moved away from me scratching his head I noticed dad looked him up and down.

"I was looking for you" I said feeling like I had done something wrong, when all I did was come down stairs to find him or Kerry.

"Hi honey, have you just woke up?" Kerry gave me a kiss on the head "let's go get a bite to eat, you must be starving. Ted will you join us?"

Ted looked surprised but I felt nervous in case he was going to say yes.

"No, no thanks, I'm supposed to meet someone" and with that he nodded in the direction of a girl with long wavy brown hair coming towards us from the bar, she was wearing a tight mid high shift dress with gold sequins and high heeled gold shiny shoes, as she walked closer holding a cocktail in her left hand I gulped as I realised it was Jessica Walsh.

"Why darling, where the hell were you?" she leaned over to give Ted a kiss and had no shame in giving him a full on snog that included a bit of tongue action! "And you stink! Why are you just standing here? Go freshen up, there are loads of people I want to introduce you to" and with that she headed back towards the bar, she looked me up and down and smiled sarcastically without saying anything. I secretly hoped she would slip on them high heels and break her leg.

"So you won't be joining us then?" said Kerry with an upbeat tone in her voice.

"No, no thanks anyway, another time" said Ted and with that he went to the elevator to go freshen up, as we walked away in the direction of a pizzeria across the hotel lobby, I couldn't help but look back at the elevator as the door was closing, I saw Ted give me a cheeky smile and a wink. It made goose pimples rise up my back, oh dear this Ted was definitely going to be a distraction!

Chapter 12

It was stifling hot, my hands were slipping holding onto the leather reins and Shamrocks was full of himself, he thought *"I'm an International Sport Horse now"* but really all he was doing was prancing around with his head high in the air and tail swishing, I found it hard to keep him focused, every mare that went by got a very manly *"nuhuhuhuhh"* which I've never heard him do before, perhaps all this Italian air was getting to him. It wasn't just Shamrocks that was feeling frisky, every time I looked at my dad he was either talking and laughing with Kerry or watching her talk and laugh to everyone else. When's he ever going to make a move?

"Molly, are you listening to me today or just here for the sunshine?" asked a very stern captain, he was stood in the middle of the collecting ring. You could hardly see him for the rising of the dry dirt from the movement of all the horses. If you have ever been to Rome, you may be aware of the crazy drivers they have, well, let me tell you that they are not a patch on their horse riders. These guys were quick, rude and dam right obnoxious. Every time I made an attempt to approach the practice jump, a rider would quickly overtake or cut in front of me, several times I had to quickly change the direction and miss the jump. This was making the captain furious. He signaled for me to stop and come towards him.

As I walked a Shamrocks towards him, I narrowly missed being knocked over by the flying Fiats with four legs and a tail! I heard the Italian girl call out some rider's names and numbers, we were last on the list.

"What's the problem O'Neil? Are you nervous?" Asked the captain as he held onto Shamrocks reins as I let go to give my arms a shake, they were hurting so much because he had been pulling like a train.

"No Captain, I'm not nervous" I said honestly "And I don't feel like I want to throw up"

"Well thank you for informing me" he said sternly "But I have one problem" he said quietly and leaned towards me to whisper something in my ear, as I leaned down from Shamrocks back to hear what he had to say. "Have you ever driven a car?"

"No, but I've moved Bills tractor a couple of time, when it was in our way in front of the paddock gate."

"I have no idea who Bill is, nor do I have any desire to know" and he leaned even closer "excuse my Italian, but if you want a shot of this you have got to feckin toughen up, do you understand?"

I nodded my head indicating I did, but then when he kept looking at me I bit my lip and told the truth "No" I had no idea what he was saying.

"I want you to get out there and bully your way to the jump, push, slide, use your whip… anything, just jump the flipping thing, or maybe this wasn't such a good idea". He stepped back and watched me.

Who does he think I am? I wasn't here for the sunshine, or to meet boys. I'll show that captain, I'll show him what me and Shamrocks can do and with that I kicked Shamrocks straight into a canter and without checking either side of me, I cantered at full speed towards the practice jump, just then out of nowhere I saw a huge polished black head with a shining silver bit clenched between his teeth, his nostrils flared pink and with a grunt Shamrocks took off to sail over the jump, just as I felt the horses black head push into my back and push me straight down off the side of Shamrocks, I could quickly see the Italian soil and I knew I was heading straight into the dirt. I felt an almighty weight hit my body from behind and then….. Nothing.

Bleep, bleep…. I could hear these sounds like it was drilling into my head, but felt absolutely still as a carrot. I tried to open my eyes but it was too difficult. I tried to lift my arms to rub my eyes but a force was keeping my arms strapped down my sides. Then as if a rush of energy I heard a familiar voice…

"Please doctor she's all I have, whatever it costs just help my little baby"

'DAD' I wanted to scream but couldn't even flicker a muscle. I felt a warmness on my right hand, and my dad whispered close to my ear "come on sweetheart, you're an O'Neil, you can do it baby." I tried and tried my hardest but it was so hard, and then finally my eye lids gave up being stapled to my head and I could see a blurry vision hovering over a bright background.

"Dad" I managed to force out the word.

"Molly my darling" I felt him come closer and hug me, Ouch it hurt all over, what was going on? "Doctor" I heard him scream and then even louder scream "DOCTOR". My eyes were so tired and I felt my body slumber back to sleep.

"Dad are you there?" I opened my eyes and stared at the ceiling above, I didn't know why I was there, or what had happened but I somehow knew that I was in hospital. I turned my head and tried to focus on the dimly lit room, I could hardly see anything so I squinted and called out again "Dad, is that you?"

The figure jumped up and came quickly to my side, as he got closer I knew it was my dad. He just grabbed my hand, I could hear him sobbing, I lifted my arm up to rub his face, it was stubbly and sticky, he was crying and could hardly get a word out, he croaked "Darling, are you ok?"

"Never been better" I tried to lift his mood, and yet I still had no idea what was happening. He held my hand to his rough face, I could feel the wet tears drench my wrist. "Stop crying Da, I'm ok…. What happened?"

"We can talk about it later pet, you just rest. Thank God and all the Angels and Saints in Heaven you're ok." He sobbed so much it made me feel sad and I started to cry myself, just then a flash came into my head, the huge black head, the flaring nostrils….I felt worried and sick and I looked at him with my heart aching to know, or did I want to know? What if he was crying for more than one reason? I shook my head, he tried to keep me calm and kept saying "shhhh, shhhh now pet just get some rest"

"Ohh no dad" I sobbed. I felt like I'd lost mum all over again. My mouth was so dry and I could hardly get a word out but I had to hear it for myself. "Is he dead?" I sobbed even louder, I felt my whole body ache all over but I didn't care, if there was no more Shamrocks then I just wanted to drift back to sleep and never wake up, never.

My dad's sobs and sniffles got quieter, he rubbed his eyes and looked at me "What the donkey?" I hated him calling him this, but I needed to know so I nodded and started to cry even more.

"Ahh pet, he's not dead….. The crafty little fecker has only gone and got himself a VIP ticket to fly back with the Captain rather than long haul with us through Europe!"

My tears turned to laughter and relief, Oh thank you God I prayed. I tried to sit up and hug my dad, he held me for a few minutes before explaining what was going on. He told me that when Shamrocks and I were jumping in the practice arena before we were to compete, that a black horse and its rider tried to cut us off, as I fell he said only that Shamrocks twisted his body and protected me from the other horse landing on top of me, I would have been as good as dead, so he had saved my life that day.

I had been in the Italian hospital for eight days, the rest of the Irish team withdrew their entries and headed home early. "The captain said, if one of our team members is fighting for her life, then we will be back another day, better and stronger".

I couldn't believe the rest of the team didn't even compete. "What about Jessica, she'll be fuming! And will take it out on me no doubt!"

"Well, you may as well know" said dad who then took a deep breath. "She was the rider on the black horse, and after her little stunt, she's got a 6 month ban, should be for life if you ask me".

"The bitch! I thought it was one of the Fiats"

"One of the what?" he asked confused.

"I'll tell you again, ohh and dad when we get home can you teach me how to drive?"

He gave me a hug and told me to rest some more. When I woke again and was seen by some doctors, they were happy to say I could go home, nothing was broken just bad bruises and my face looked like I had been in the wars.

Outside the hospital waiting for me to get out of the

wheelchair was Kerry, she had a huge smile and a beautiful bunch of roses for me. Nobody had ever given me flowers before. She gave me a huge hug, it still hurt all over but I was so glad to see her.

"Where's the jeep and box?" I asked.

"Well well well, let me tell you... you know that young dish" she licked her lips and widened her eyes "Ted., well as soon as you fell off Shamrocks, he was right over to you, before anyone else, sorted out Shamrocks, made sure he got all the best treatment, drove our jeep and box back across Europe!"

Holy cow, I thought. This is big. I only spoke to him twice in my life and he's done all this. My dad's eyes were narrowing more and more as Kerry talked.

"And he's been calling four to five times a day to see how you are... so what do you think of all that?"

"What do I think?" I was speechless, "I'll have to send him a thank you card"

"hmmm hmmm" she replied "I think you and me need a girly weekend".

My dad just shook his head and carried my bag towards a taxi that was to take us to the airport and back home again. I couldn't wait to see Shamrocks again. I didn't want Kerry to feel upset so I whispered to my dad when she was trying to translate to the taxi driver "Airporto por favor!" and stretched out her arms to signal an airplane.

"Can we stop at mum's grave when we are in Dublin?"

"Off course you can pet, anytime you like" said dad kissing the top if my head. We both looked at Kerry and then burst out laughing at her.

Chapter 13

The sun blinded my eyes as I walked along the silent path towards my mum's grave. It was a warm afternoon and the sunset was softly lowering, tall shadows from high headstones relieved my sight for a few seconds while I tried to locate where mum was resting. I can remember the funeral director giving me a choice of grave locations, not something you want to do all alone at 14 years old. Either beside the busy road or at the quiet end that looked onto the mountains, I chose the quieter end hoping it would have been what she would have liked. Some graves looked lonely and sad, very old graves made me shiver, some people say that if you shiver, someone is passing over your grave and at the moment I had a horrible feeling as I looked around, but luckily I saw nobody else in this grave yard!

As I got closer to the pretty headstone I felt very sad, the saddest I had felt in a long while. Dad and Kerry promised to stay at the gate, I didn't want the drama of them seeing me get upset, and I needed to be alone. Even though I knew my mum was lying deep down under the ground, lifeless and dead, I somehow felt very close to her once more.

Her grave had the heading "In memory of Molly Doyle, loving mum of Molly O'Neil and adored by everyone". I could tell my aunt Annie had been visiting regular as she promised. There were beautiful pink and yellow flowers growing neatly in the bright green grass that lay over her. A little white picket fence surrounded her that reminded me of the fence we had around Shamrocks paddock. I knelt down on the grass and touched the ground, expecting it to be cold and sad but instead it felt warm and comforting. I looked around again making sure nobody could hear me;

"Hi mum" I said slowly, a slow breeze went by that made me smile, maybe it was just the wind but in my head I felt like it was her, so I took a deep breath and continued.

"Suppose you know all about Shamrocks, sure aren't you looking down over me all the time? And you know about my fall in Italy.... I'm ok, nothing wrong apart from the fact I'll probably never get selected to ride again, sure it was a nice little holiday and I got to take the donkey too, Oh No!, now I'm calling him a donkey, don't tell dad"

I looked around again just to make sure nobody heard.

"I hope heaven is nice mum. Don't be sad for me, I'm ok now. Dad is great and I think he likes Kerry, I know you would like her too, she's really nice. She does my hair and stuff, not as good as you but I'll never say"

"There's this boy, his name is Ted, well I call him 'Mr Distraction' he's kind of nice, he's going out with a total nutcase though. I'm not sure how I feel about him, I don't know if you know this but I may as well tell you, I have kissed someone before, it was the time I went to Megan's sleepover and I kissed her brother, it was horrible, I want to forget it but somehow can't, anyway I'm not sure why I'm telling you, I know you would just say 'play it cool, and he'll come running!" I smiled at my own thoughts of what she might say, I rubbed the grass and leaned down to give it a kiss, I put my head down and whispered "I love you mum, I love you very much and every time I ride, I think of you." I felt a little tear start to roll down the side of my face and into my ear, I didn't want to cry again, I tried to feel strong so instead I smiled and said "not really the diet you wanted to go on, was it mum?" I got up and touched the grass once more and bowed my head and said three Hail Mary's, three Glory Be to the Father and three Our Fathers. I kissed the headstone and whispered "Love you mum, talk to you when I'm on Shamrocks again" and turned to head for dad and Kerry.

Poor Kerry, she is a softy I thought. There she was, in my dad's arms crying her eyes out.

"Come here baby" she sobbed. I took out a tissue and gave it to her to wipe her black smudged mascara running eyes and snuffle nose. "Are you OK hun?"

"I'm fine, honest I am" I said as we hugged.

"It's just so sad, you and your mum were so close, and I know how hard this is for you, and I think you must be the bravest little girl, I mean young woman, I have ever seen in my life, and I just need to tell you, that I love you very much and that I will always be here for you no matter what, ok"

Oh no, I had done so well going to the grave and been so strong not crying, now I couldn't help it, the water works started to flow, I was more sad for Kerry than anything else.

"OK" I choked as I hugged her tight. I felt dad's arms cover us both.

"Come here you two" he said in a deep voice. "Let's not be upset, and let's get back on track and show the world who Molly O'Neil and Shamrocks are, and do your mother proud"

"Molly, Shamrocks, Dad, Mum and Kerry proud" I smiled at Kerry as she touched her heart in appreciation that I hadn't left her out.

"Right lets hit the road lads" as we walked over to the jeep before setting back to Clada.

As we got into the jeep dad checked I was ok and Kerry wiped her eyes and stretched back from the front seat to hold my hand, the warmth in her eyes were genuine and I knew I had another mission ahead.... To make sure she was to be my stepmom.

Chapter 14

I was so happy to see Shamrocks, he was in his stable tucked up for the night when we arrived home, but he had heard the jeep coming through the village and was whinnying loudly. I jumped out of the jeep before my dad had turned off the engine and ran to his stable, opened the bolt as quick as I could, he held his head in tight around my back as I hugged him tightly around his large muscular neck.

"You OK?" I asked him concerned. "I've missed you so much, and I thought you were dead, I'll never ride you so stupidly again I promise" I suddenly jumped out of my skin when I heard a voice say:

"Your weren't riding stupidly, in fact I think your probably the most talented rider I have ever seen"

Who was that? I stretched over to turn on the stable light, with that, the stranger in the dark did the same thing and we touched hands which made me jump and pull my hand away. He turned on the switch and the fluorescent light flickered a few seconds over the old stable before coming on. I gasped and looked completely shocked as there standing in the night light was the one and only, Ted.

"What are you doing here?" I asked completely, shocked, mortified that I was standing in front of him with two day old greasy hair and another silly slogan t-shirt that Kerry had got me, this time saying 'Red is the new blond'. I tried to fix my hair a little by running my fingers through it and looking down, I thought my top was a bit too revealing for my liking.

"Well someone had to watch over your little man until you got home" He talked so softly it made my arms go all goose bumpy!

"Thanks, but you needn't have stayed, Bill would have looked after him" with that, the back door to our pub opened and out walked a drunken Bill singing 'Show me the way to go home… I'm tired and I wanna go to bed'

Ted raised one eyebrow and smirked "As I said, after meeting the trust worthy Bill and saw how he put Shamrocks into the paddock full of cows, I quickly decided to stay over for a few days, anyway I like it here, got to know a few neighbours"

I know I shouldn't have said what I was about to say, but since I met Ted, and he seemed like a really nice guy and not the show off some of the other riders I met have been, I couldn't believe he was dating that trollop, Jessica Walsh! "And I suppose your close to your girlfriend too, so that's convenient for you" I said, waiting for his reply. He looked a little upset, perhaps I came out with that a little too harsh and maybe he thought it was none of my business to even ask anything about his love affairs. He took a deep breath and just as he opened his mouth, a hand touched his shoulder as in walked my dad.

"How are ye Ted?" he asked him shaking his hand "I don't know how to thank you, driving Shamrocks home and taking good care of him an all"

"Ahh no problem Martin, anytime." He replied. He looked back at me and then gave a nod as headed out the stable door "I'll be off now, maybe see you all soon I hope."

"Hang on, hang on, you can't just leave now" exclaimed dad "sure why don't you come in for some grub and a few pints, and sure stay another night and get on the road tomorrow."

"Thanks Martin but I better be off, glad your all ok and say my good byes to Kerry for me" and with that he walked over to his silver jeep and drove away in the direction of Dublin.

Dad stood in the twilight of the night and waved after Ted as he left, then turned scratching his head and headed back into the stable. "That's weird, he spends the last three weeks caring for this donkey and won't even spend one more night so we can show him our appreciation" He patted Shamrocks on the neck and rubbed all his legs checking they were all ok after travelling. "Sure maybe he's gone to see his girlfriend" he said standing up and looking at me.

I felt so mad. His girlfriend that cow with the big house and big horse truck and everything shiny and new, sure why would somebody like Ted be remotely interested in a nobody like me? The thoughts in my head upset me so much that I looked at my dad with anger in my eyes before fleeing from the stable.

"Women!" is what I heard dad say to shamrocks as I was walking away "They never know when their happy"

I went straight upstairs to my bedroom where I closed the door, and sulked holding Bobo until I fell asleep.

I woke to the sound of birds chirping outside, opening my eyes the sun was shining in through the window, I was tucked up in bed and realised that dad must have tucked me in last night. I felt foolish for being upset over some silly boy…. What was it dad had said only yesterday, had I forgotten already… show the world who we are, and that's what I intended to do.

"I'll show them" I said out loud and decided that there was no time to waste as I jumped up out of bed, put on a fresh pair of jodhpurs and clean top and skipped down the stairs to see Shamrocks.

Outside dad had Shamrocks in the yard and was hosing down his steaming hot body, why was he so steamy? What was going on?

"What's wrong with him?" I asked very concerned as I ran over and hugged him, soaking my top and his sloppy wet neck smothered my face as he tried to scratch himself off me.

"Good morning to you too" said dad with a big grin. "There's nothing wrong with him, in fact, I have good news, no I have great news…"

"What?" I asked anxious.

He just kept smiling and said nothing.

"DAD!" I shouted "What's going on?" He was trying me now… really trying!

"Well, after you went to bed last night, I called the Captain to let him know you were back and everything was fine, and he asked me would be fit to travel next week, so I said yeah, shouldn't be a problem" he walked over to turn off the hose, I followed him and Shamrocks who had no head collar on followed after me. Dad turned over a bucket and sat down in the sunshine. "Where's Kerry with me bacon sandwich gone?" he said casually, I walked closer and stood in his sunlight.

"Travel to where?" I asked him. As if wanting to know himself, Shamrocks walked over to, blocking all the sunlight out.

He smiled. He stood up slowly then grabbed me as he swung me around in circles.

"DAD, put me down, are you gone mad or something? What's going on?" I screamed.

"What's going on? You my little darling, will be travelling VIP all expenses paid with Mr Shamrock a.k.a The Donkey to West Palm Beach, Florida to compete and represent Ireland at the Florida International Horse Show"

"Ohh my God" I said slowly then a bit louder "Ohh My God" this time I screamed it "Ohh my GOD" I hugged Shamrocks and kissed him smack on the nose. "So why's he all sweaty?"

"Because he needs to be in top shape and we need to get to work" he was smiling so much it made my heart jumped with joy for him.

"But dad, what about the pub? Can we afford it?" I was worried for quite some time, ever since I saw him doing the books that day with Kerry. I remember it because it was the first day I laid eyes on Shamrocks. I noticed he looked worried every time a bill came through the door and sometimes the pub was closed a bit too early in the evening because there was no custom.

"Don't you be worrying about them things, sure, things are a little tight at the moment but something will turn up, God is good to us, remember that" he stroked my cheek and headed towards the pub shouting "Kerry, where's me sandwich? "

I couldn't believe it! Florida International Horse Show, me, Molly O'Neil who only started to ride seven months ago was now picked to ride for Ireland in America, I had never been to America and knew Disney World was in Florida, but best not to mention anything like that to dad as he probably couldn't afford it. I walked Shamrocks through the village to dry him off, stopping outside Mrs Hegarty's shop, I could see her run from the back probably to say hello I thought, but instead she was waving a brush

"Get that mule out of here" she said franticly.

"Mrs Hegarty, he's no mule, we've just been selected to jump in America" I said excitedly and feeling over the moon.

"Sure that means nothing, didn't you travel to Italy and fall before you even did one jump, so don't be coming here and tying that mule up outside, God knows he probably has fleas! Go on, away with ye..." she shouted as she waved her sweeping brush in the air after us.

How rude I thought, she was right about the whole Italy not jumping saga though… hopefully that will never happen again, or I'll jump into the Atlantic and let sharks eat me!

"Come on Shamrocks" I said making sure she heard "time to d-flea you" and we headed back towards our pub once more, Shamrocks followed and nudged my back every few strides as if to tell me there was not to worry about anything.

Chapter 15

Flags were blowing gently in the breeze, the warm heat was suffocating, and the air was so hot to breathe, it made Shamrocks have sweaty patches behind his ears all the time. We weren't allowed to walk around the show grounds with him not having a head collar and lead on, I tried several different routes to the wash bays to cool him off, each time a security guy on a bike came gliding beside us with his walkie-talkie squawking 'tell the Irish, collar and lead or we'll have them disqualified' and 'roger that' replied the security guy.

"I know, I know, collar and lead" I would say to the guy on the bike to put his mind at rest. "Sorry Shamrocks, we're not in Clada now".

It seemed like a long time after arriving at the showground before it was our turn to jump. Competitions commenced at 6.30am and I would watch them all day long and even take Shamrocks out of his stable and sit on his back and just watch the competitions for hours. We were to jump on the Friday evening in what's called an International Welcome, it was going to be a one round speed and I watched every rider and their techniques to see if I could gain any tips.

Kerry spent her days by the hotel swimming pool, topping up her tan. Dad said she had to be, the worst groom in history and didn't know why we brought her… again!

Friday evening arrived and so did the Captain. He looked completely different in shorts and flip flops. He walked the course with me and told me exactly how I should ride it, I was starting to feel nervous again and could feel sick coming up and down my throat. My other team members were not so nervous, they laughed and joked with other International riders that I had only ever seen on the television before, I couldn't believe I was actually going to compete amongst them!

The Captain told me to sit in the rider stands while dad kept Shamrocks walking around, when he joined me he produced a hip flask.

"Take this" he gestured giving me the narrow silver flask.

"What is it?" I asked curiously.

"It'll help, one big swig and it will stop that vomit coming up" he took my hand and made me take it from him. I put the tankard to my lips, I could smell the strong whiskey stench and closed my eyes tightly as it sent shivers down my spine and the burning sensation on my lips as the alcohol went down my throat making my mouth sting.

"Agggg" I screamed handing him back the flask.

"Shhh, keep it down" and he quickly hid the flask in the back pocket of his shorts. "Now you know the course?" he asked, I nodded, I knew it inside out, upside down and backwards. "Just ride like you always do, don't let the circumstances that surround you, change you, do you understand?"

"I'm not sure" I said honestly, because I honestly wasn't sure!

"Look, relax, take deep breaths and don't be nervous or Shamrocks will be too, ok?" he asked.

"OK" I lied, I had no clue what he was on about, when he talked about horses he was brilliant, but when he tried to communicate with humans… that's when he struggled.

As I mounted Shamrocks I gave him a huge hug before taking up the reins, just then dad stretched up and touched my hand, he didn't need to say anything I could see it in his eyes and I don't know if it was pure courage or the whiskey but I suddenly felt inner power and the nerves faded and confidence took over. I gave him a wink and turned Shamrocks to begin our warm up regime, I listened to the Captains voice intensively and followed his instructions. I was secretly happy to make it over the first practice jump this time!

Fifteen minutes later it was time. The Captain tightened Shamrocks girth and left me with dad before I entered the arena. I was the final rider in the class.

"Molly" said dad as I was just about to go in "You can do it sweetheart" and he blew me a kiss as I trotted off into the arena, I turned back once and blew him a kiss back.

Here I was. Alone. This has to be the loneliest place in the world, flags blew, music played, children screamed, generators from stands hummed and television cameras and photographers monitored our every move, the American commentator was in the center of the arena and it was courtesy to bow before starting.

The judge stood up with his big cowboy hat and gave me a salute to start. The bell rang and without hesitation I shortened my reins and Shamrocks and I were on our way to our first jump.

I approached it exactly as the Captain had said and Shamrocks lifted higher than ever and in between the jumps we needed to be quick so we galloped fast, and when possible even faster. We flew around the course taking tight turns and jumping at angles that hadn't been tested before. I could see our final jump, it was a very wide fence in red, blue and white representing the USA, I gave Shamrocks a loose rein and stood up in my stirrups and kicked him into a flat out gallop as we came thundering down to the jump, I could hear the massive crowd roar with horror and I shut my eyes as I could see that we were a long way off from takeoff, but up, up, up and up and over Shamrocks lifted. I opened my eyes and we touched the other side, I tried to gather my reins but they caught in Shamrocks legs while we were in the air, so I used his neck to push myself back into the saddle and we galloped through the finish line with no reins…..

Silence fell as I rode through the finish and heard the American cowboy shout from his PA system that flooded the arena.

"Holy smokes ladies and gentlemen, that has set a new record and clear with the quickest God dam time I have ever seen in my life. And the winner by over ten seconds is the little Irish girl on her little Irish grey, Molly O'Neil and Shamrocks."

I didn't stop cantering as I rode straight out of the arena to find my dad. The crowd were cheering and waving at Shamrocks and I. Kerry came running from the stands with her video camera hanging from her arm, she screamed my name so I could hear her.

"Kerry" I screamed back to her as she came running over and threw her arms around the drenching neck of a very hot Shamrocks "Where's dad?" I needed to see him and couldn't see him from all the well-wishers that were gathering around us. A sash was being put around my body and a rug over Shamrocks to wear for the presentation. But where was my dad? The steward was signaling for me to enter the arena for the presentation but I didn't want to go in, not without seeing dad, so I stood up on my saddle to see over the crowd and there in the corner of the practice arena was dad looking straight at me with floods of tears. I started to cry and nearly lost my balance. I put my arms out to him as if I was only three years old, I needed my dad more than anything in the world and I wanted to share the excitement and joy with him. With that he ran towards me, pushing through the crowd and stumbling until he reached me, I jumped off my saddle once he got closer and straight into his arms for the biggest hug I had ever got in my life. We held each other closely until he looked straight in my eyes with all the pride in the world.

"Told you, you could do it" he whispered.

"Molly O'Neil, if you don't enter the arena now you WILL be disqualified!" said the steward once more. Just then the Captain joined us with pats on our backs and told me to skedaddle or else!

As I rode into the arena I looked at mums charm bracelet on my wrist and gave it a little kiss, I knew she was with me, looking down and smiling.

It wasn't our only victory at the West Palm Beach showground's. We clocked up another two wins, and third on the final day in the Grand Prix. The success guaranteed us a chance at boot camp…. Well that's what I called it. It was a selection of twelve horse and rider combinations to attend the Olympic trials with the Captain and other judges. This stared only three days after we returned home from America and it also meant that I had to stay over for a week without dad or Kerry whilst I trained.

On other matters, the whole dad and Kerry saga was not going as I hoped. I tried a few times to let them have dinner together alone or go swimming together but they just seem to stay as best friends.

Another plan of action would have to be put in place I decided, this I was calling operation step-mom!

Chapter 16

There was a quite nervous energy in the Olympic training camp. It was held at a magnificent stud farm in the County of Kildare, I had never seen such a beautiful yard. It was run by one of the selectors who lived in the massive mansion that was owned by a sheikh.

I slept in my own room in a wing off the mansion that was shared with eleven other riders. They all seemed intimidating when they spoke about their years and years of experience, and numerous victories around the world, as they drank wine and beer in the evening. I was too young to drink alcohol and dad had warned me not to do anything stupid that could jeopardise my chances of making it to the London Olympics. Jessica's ban was lifted for the occasion and she too joined us with her presence and to my astonishment Ted seemed to keep his distance with her. This, she took out on me.

The first morning when I got up to get dressed I could not find my riding boots which mysteriously turned up in the manure heap. It took me ages to get them cleaned up and I was late entering the arena on Shamrocks, this did not impress some of the selectors. Another day, I was taking a long shower and when I came out my clothes and towel was missing from where I had left them hanging, I found them on my bed in my bedroom, after I raced down the hallway, wet, humiliated and freezing cold. I just made it to my room as I heard some skittering and laughter. It made me feel upset but I was stronger than them. So, instead of slumping down to cry I quickly dressed myself and walked down the hallway passing an open bedroom door to Jessica's room. I stopped and gave a big smile as I popped my head in the doorway;

"Hi guys, just to let you know I won't be joining you all for tea, the Captain has invited me to meet the Sheikh for dinner" I could see their stupid faces drop as I continued "I better dash, thanks for putting my clothes out for me" And I turned to head down the winding staircase before hearing a few comments like, "she's lying" or "the sheikhs not even here" or "why does she get to go?" Of course I was making the whole thing up; I thought I would head down to the stables and spend the evening with Shamrocks. I was feeling a little hungry and when I reached Shamrocks stable I couldn't help feel upset and lonely.

"Hey you" I said to him as he gave me a

whinny with his ears pricked, a huge warm welcome as always. "Did you enjoy your tea?" I asked him and checked his water bowl was clean, and got a pitch fork to give his stable a quick muck out. I was chatting away to him as I always did when we were alone and then suddenly I jumped a mile when I heard;

"Do you always talk to yourself?" It was Ted. He was wearing a white polo shirt and jeans. I looked away quickly and didn't stare too long, or least I hoped I hadn't.

"I wasn't talking to myself, I was talking to Shamrocks" I said and gave Shamrocks another quick cuddle. "Why do you keep sneaking up on me anyway? And how come you're not having dinner with the others?"

"Why aren't you having dinner with the Captain and Sheikh?" he replied sarcastically.

"Well, I was too, but I thought Shamrocks needed the company more" I replied biting my bottom lip and continued to muck out Shamrocks stable.

"Bullshit" said Ted. It made me stop and look right at him. He was right of course, anyway it was none of his business what I was doing, why didn't he just go back to the house and do his own thing. "You hungry?" he asked.

"Maybe" I said quietly, I was actually starving. I had not eaten since the night before.

"Come on, I'll take you for a good feed, you'll need your energy tomorrow" said Ted as he put his hand out in gesture for me to come with him. I gave Shamrocks another hug and when Ted turned his back I gave Shamrocks a quick kiss on the lips. Ted turned around but hopefully he didn't see me do it!

"Where we going?" I asked curiously following his fast paced walk and not sure where I was heading.

"I know a quiet place that has the best fish and chips you have ever tasted" said Ted smiling at my scurried walk.

"And where is it? How will we get there?" I wasn't sure if I should go with him.

"I'm a big boy, I have a car, remember?" and he took out a set of keys from his pocket and a silver jeep bleeped signaling where it was. He opened the passenger door and I jumped in, at least he had manners I thought. I watched him as he walked around to hop into the driver's side and my heart gave a few extra beats, I reminded myself that I was playing with fire here and that he was Mr Distraction, and not to let anything happen, just dinner…

We drove out into the country side, it was just starting to rain a little and we talked about the ground for tomorrow morning, I didn't quite understand some of the terms he used so I would just nod and look out the window.

"So where you from, you know… in Dublin, what part?" he asked after the small talk.

"Smithfield" I said, trying not show my strong Dublin accent too much. He smiled and began to laugh a little. "What's so funny?" I asked.

"Nothing" he said and smirked again, so I asked him once more and was starting to feel a little annoyed. "Well, it's just, not many fifteen year old girls from Smithfield get the chance to ride at the Olympics"

"As opposed to someone who lives in a huge white mansion and has mummy and daddy at their every beck and call?" I sounded a little bitchy but I thought it rude of him to make assumptions about my upbringing.

"I'm sorry, I'm sorry" He said looking sincere "I didn't mean to offend you, it's just some of us were wondering how we never heard of you before three months ago, and now here you are, very close to the biggest event in show jumping, and you have just come back from Florida, with a couple of descend wins under your belt" He swallowed and looked straight ahead as he continued "Do you know the Captain well?"

"What do you mean?" I asked.

"Is he like an uncle or something? Because there is no way you have only learned to ride and come this far in such a little time" he said.

"No" I answered "I'm not related, my dad taught me everything I know, and it turns out, he must know a lot".

"And your mum?" he said "I've not seen her around.

"You won't" I wasn't sure if I wanted to tell him.

"Why not?" Ted asked confused why I was not mentioning her.

"Because she's not around, hard to get in touch with" I knew I was digging myself deeper but

I didn't want to tell him.

"Sorry, didn't mean to pry" he said as he turned left off the motorway and into a thatched roof pub that had a huge toucan Guinness bird outside. I was so used to all the Irish slogans and bric-a-bracs from dad's pub but this place was really cool, perhaps dad should visit here to get some ideas and maybe attract more customers.

We ordered the fish and chips, Ted had a Guinness and I had a coke. I thought the food would never come and when it did I ate so fast I was finished before him.

"So, do you have a boyfriend?" He asked with a little smile.

"No, I've no time for anything like that" I replied. "Have you?"

"Got a boyfriend?" he said "No, no, not really my thing!" he laughed at his own joke.

"You know what I mean… girlfriend?" I asked again.

"No, I've no time for anything like that" he said and gave me a smile before taking another sip of his pint. "You don't look fifteen"

"I'll be sixteen in two weeks" I said.

"Sweet sixteen" mimicked Ted. "And never been kissed" and he looked for my reaction.

"Ohh I've been kissed, more than you could imagine" I answered.

"Seriously?" he quizzed "With whom?" He seemed a bit upset now which I quickly decided was a very good thing, perhaps he was interested in me after all.

"A boy" I said.

"What boy?" Ted wanted to know.

"Well, you've met him. In fact, you travelled with him from Italy" I said and watched his face change to a smile.

"The donkey" he said.

"Don't call him that, it really upsets him" I replied, truth was, it upset me! "And what's the story with you and Miss Walsh?"

"That story has truly ended" he said "I don't want to talk about her, she's a conniving, sarcastic, two faced stuck up cow"

"Couldn't have put it better me self" I

replied as we made a toast with each other.

"So young O'Neil, in two weeks' time can I meet you for a birthday drink?" he asked taking another big swig out of his pint that was just finished.

"Are you asking me out on a date Mr Brown?" I asked.

"Maybe, or even just to get to know you a little better?" he said.

"Yeah sure, I'll eh… be in Dublin I think" I was feeling a little nervous, how could I tell dad about this and how will I get a chance to see him alone in Dublin? I would figure it out…

He took out his mobile phone "Give me your number and I'll text you" he said. After giving him my number I went to the bar to pay for our meal and drinks, with that, Ted realised what I was doing and insisted that he paid.

"I have never had a woman try pay for me before" he said. Thoughts were starting to come into my head, I'd pay for him! I could smell his after shave as we stood close to each other at the busy bar. After paying and on our way out the door which was hard to reach in the crowded little bar, I felt him grab my hand and take me across the car park. The heavens had opened and we were getting pretty wet, my white t-shirt was damp and clinging to my body. He opened the door for me then ran around to his side. We both laughed at how wet our clothes were, he stared at me for a moment then stretched his arm out. He leaned closer and I was just about to close my eyes for our first kiss when I noticed he was stretching into the back seat in which he then produced a towel for me to dry my long wet red hair. I felt so foolish that for a split second I thought Ted Brown was going to sneak me my first official kiss.

"Thanks" I said shyly, hoping he hadn't noticed what I just did. I dried my hair as we drove off back to camp in the rain. On our return he dropped me back at the courtyard entrance as I wanted to check on Shamrocks before going to bed. I secretly hoped he was going to park his car and follow me into the stable for a snog but after waiting ten minutes it was clear that it was not going to happen.

When I arrived back into the house, I could hear talk from the living room. As I entered you could smell the alcohol and the room was cloudy with smoke from cigarettes. Jessica was in the middle of a sofa between two other guys who no doubt were competing to be her next flavour! Then I suddenly saw Ted, he was sat on an armchair and gave me a wink when nobody was looking.

"So where exactly have you been Molly?" asked Murt, a guy from Yawl in Cork who had won many major Irish championships. He had curly brown hair and a few teeth missing in the front of his mouth and talked with a little lisp.

"I was er…" and trying to think of something, Ted spoke up and saved the day.

"I heard the chopper land, did you get wet running all that way from the helipad?" said Ted. I looked at him as if he had two heads, what was he on about?

"You were in the sheikhs chopper?" said Jessica with her mouth nearly touching the ground. I was about to put the record straight when Murt suddenly started.

"Why the feckin hell did you get to have a go in the chopper and not us?" he asked in a high pitched voice that can only be described as a toddler having a tantrum.

"Because she's probably shagging him" said Jessica staring at me.

"But sure isn't the sheikh married?" said Murt confused.

"What planet are you from, he has hundreds of wives" said Jessica looking pretty peed off!

"So are you marrying the sheikh then?" asked Murt.

"Oh for God's sake Murt, shut up!" said Ted getting to his feet. "We have an early start tomorrow and I suggest we all get some shut eye". And he grabbed my arm and escorted me to the kitchen and out of ear shot from the others. We both looked at each other and burst out laughing.

"Go to bed, you need to rest, I'll see you in the morning" and leaned forward and kissed me on the forehead. It was a little bit like a kiss my dad would give, but at least he was sweet.

"Night Ted" I gave him a little wave as I skipped up the winding staircase, I could feel his eyes on me and just as I got to the top I turned and saw him give me a little wave before going back into the room of smog. I shut my bedroom door and did a little dance on the spot with excitement.... Then I remembered, he was Mr Distraction and I tried to think about the day ahead, but found it very difficult and hardly got any sleep at all that night.

Chapter 17

It was 4.30am and I sat on the edge of my little single bed, I had chosen beige jodhpurs and an emerald green turtle neck sweater to wear for the final days, Olympic training day. Shamrocks had been a star all week but he showed some signs of fatigue, as it wasn't long since our trip from Florida.

There was a tiny pitter patter of rain on the window pane, I could see the roof of the courtyard from my bedroom window and it looked dark and the moon light bounced off the wet tiled roof. I wanted to go see Shamrocks before anyone else had arrived but I didn't want to disturb his slumber either, we both needed to be on top form. It's funny I thought, as I sat there on the little bed fiddling with mums charm bracelet around and around my wrist, that it's not even a year and half since I was on a bus with my ipod thinking about some random boy or what I would buy at the weekend, when all I want now and all that I could think of and hope for, was a chance to be on the team that would represent Ireland at the 2012 London Olympics.

I couldn't stay in my room any longer. I had remembered over hearing that the course of jumps were being built last night. So I made my way down to the grass paddock to have a look and learn the course. Today's session was going to be treated as a competition, so no tuition, no advice, just me and Shamrocks.

I was wearing my yellow mac with the hood up. The ground was soft from the night's rain. I decided that I should put studs in Shamrocks shoes today, his high heels as Kerry called them. The course was big, colourful and terrifying. I was no longer feeling sick and scared but I did feel lonely. I walked the course three times, double checking all the distances and tried to remember, everything dad had taught me. Where there were five strides I knew little Shamrocks would do six strides and for the double, we would have to go helter skelter if we were going to even be close to taking off for the second element. I spotted a small wooden shelter, presumably this was for the selectors to sit and keep dry in today's observation. I was on a cold bench going over the course out loud and talking to myself which, I sometimes did when I was sure nobody was around.

"OK, so two to three is a long four strides.... After that double we have a quick shortening to do before the big feckin planks...."

"For you my dear, I recommend you don't get too close to the.. feckin planks.." said a man's voice from behind the shelter. I jumped off my seat and pulled my hood down. Did I hear a voice or was this God talking to me, I couldn't see anyone around and I looked up into the sky at the falling rain. Was I going mad? So I asked out loud:

"Is that you God?" Then from behind the shelter came a man dressed in a white sheet with a red turban around his head, I took a few steps back in complete and utter shock! I blinked a couple of times in the pouring rain, my hair was saturated from the pouring rain and the strangers eyes locked into mine as he watched me back off and tremble. "Oh Shit… Is it you". With that the man smiled and put his hand out to shake mine.

"Some people have actually called me God." said the deep broken, foreign voice. "But my name is Sheikh Mumbossa" and stood waiting for me to shake his hand back. I felt so stupid; I lowered my head and walked towards him in shame. I didn't know what to do so I stretched out to shake his hand and then for some strange reason, I genuflected like you would do in church. "So you must be Molly O'Neil" he said with amusement at my unusual greeting.

"Nice to meet you sir" I answered "I am so sorry about before, I thought nobody was around" I tried to run some rain off the top of my head to make myself look a bit more presentable, he was a Sheikh after all, which meant king... right? I wasn't sure.

"That's OK Miss Molly, I sometimes like to talk and think out loud too, it's healthy" he said reassuring me that I was not nuts, or silly. "I noticed you walked your course many times, and before anyone else in your camp, why is this?" he demanded in his broken Arabic accent.

"Well, I couldn't sleep. And I'm trying to remember what my dad would tell me if he were here" I looked over at the planks, this was the one line I wasn't sure, should I go easy or should I go fast. The Sheikh nodded in interest and then surprised me when he said;

"I walk it short; your little horse will struggle with the height. So perhaps take my advice... go for it!" and he gave me a wink before taking out his cell phone and spoke in Arabic to someone and within seconds a boy came running from the house with two umbrellas.

"Go freshen up Miss Molly, and I wish you every luck, I will be very happy to hear good news that you have done well today" He handed me an umbrella and with that he walked off quickly with the boy who came from the house, running behind him to keep up as he got extremely wet whilst shading the Sheikh from the rain with the umbrella over his head. It was starting to get light so I walked in the rain, with my new umbrella towards the courtyard. Shamrocks could hear me coming before he even saw me. His whinny made me smile, and when I turned the corner he waved his head up and down and kicked the bottom half of his door in excitement. I don't think he enjoyed being so confided to his stable but I had to explain to him that we weren't in Clada now and he had to calm down. He certainly wasn't nervous about today's trial as he guzzled down his food. I plaited his main neatly and put the studs in his shoes. My tack was gleaming as always and as the others were strolling into the yard after their breakfast as I was leading Shamrocks out of his stable to commence warming him up slowly.

"Bit too eager, are we O'Neil?" asked Murt as he scratched his curly head. Jessica who was walking brazenly behind him just looked at her watch and smirked at me.

"You need to walk the course first, no help today, or no daddy to run to either" she said sarcastically. She made my blood boil, but I was better than her, so I bit my lip and instead of biting back with a rude comment that would only have me lower myself to her level, I turned to face her.

"Been raining all night, best you use studs today… wouldn't want you to have a nasty accident or anything" Murt clapped his hands and applauded at my comment. Jessica just turned and stomped towards her mares stable who had her ears flat back against her beautiful black velvet neck. She was such a fabulous mare and unfortunately for her, she ended up in the hands of Jessica. God knows what poor Shamrocks had been through with her in the past, luckily I don't think he remembered.

I warmed up slowly and well. I blanked out all thoughts and concentrated on the course in hand. The Captain walked slowly into the center of the warming up paddock with a sheet of paper in his hand.

"OK children listen up…. This is it. The final chance for each of you to show us if you have what it takes. This is the order you will jump in, due to the weather conditions, one round only. Anyone want to back out, then please say so now" he looked at each of us slowly without smiling "Good, good" he continued "As we had said before, one round only and please put your horse away and we will all meet tonight at 6.00pm sharp and some of you, will not be continuing, and the remainder… will be under my wing for the next three months until we go see the Queen, and Big Ben and all that malarkey!" Everyone gave a more relaxed giggle. "Good luck everyone" he finished and made his way back to the wooden hut with four other judges and selectors. I looked at the list… I was first to go. It can be two things to go first. One, you get it done and it's over with, you either do well or fail completely. On the other hand, you don't get to see anyone else jump and this could mean missing something important about the course.

We had no time to lose. I popped Shamrocks over a few jumps, keeping him calm and energetic. I looked at the Captain at the side of the arena, he stood up and waved his arms indicating for me to enter and start the round. I trotted in and halted in front of all the selectors and bowed. They bowed back. I took a few strides walking backwards and proceeded into a medium paced canter. "OK Shamrocks, this is it" and I shortened my reins and we approached the first jump. Shamrocks was a little unsure of the wet ground and the studs in his shoes but he took control and brought me safely to the other side, we continued to fence two, three, four and then the big double. I asked for another gear and he lengthened his stride as we went extremely fast to the first element and quickly pop, pop over each jump. Instead of steadying for the planks I used the advice of the Sheikh, and galloped at full speed towards it. As I got closer I realised it may not be such a good idea and I closed my eyes and screamed as we took off.... Time seemed to stay still.... Thud, we landed the other side, I checked behind me and the planks were swinging on the flat cups attached to the wings. Keep swinging but don't fall down, I thought... just don't fall... please don't fall. We had two more jumps to go and we popped, popped and through the finish. I glanced over at the planks, they were at the very edge of the cups and had not fallen. I smiled at an image that came into my head... mum's ghost standing there, holding the edge of the plank preventing it from falling.

I stretched down and hugged Shamrocks and kissed his neck all over. Ted was standing at the entrance to the arena with a handful of grass, just like dad would have done.

"That was amazing" said Ted "No matter what... you are one cool kid!"

"Good luck Ted" I said honestly, I hoped he would do well. I was so happy with our performance I trotted Shamrocks all the way back to the courtyard and jumped off and headed straight to the phone to ring dad and Kerry to tell them how we did.

The phone rang one ring and dad answered with "Molly?"

"DAD" I shouted "We went clear, can you believe it… he was amazing, he sailed over everything" I was so ecstatic I couldn't get the words out quick enough.

"How did the others do?" asked dad. I could hear Kerry in the background, wanting to know what I was saying and dad telling her to shush!

"I don't know" I answered

"What do you mean?" he said curiously.

"I was first to go, and I came straight back to the yard to ring you" I answered. I suddenly just realised that I had no idea how anyone else was doing.

"Un-tack and run back as fast as you can…" he instructed "Oh and Molly baby… you're doing great pet".

"Thanks dad, say hi to Kerry" and I hung up, un-tacked Shamrocks and rode him bare back to watch the others. It was raining heavier and I had a rug over Shamrocks hind quarters and wrapped it around us both. The other riders came and went, all sliding into jumps, knocking fences and swearing that the conditions were unfair. Jessica was going clear until the planks, they crumbled down like building blocks, was my mum still standing there I chuckled to myself without anyone noticing! Ted looked nervous and concentrated on the task ahead. He took his little bay mare around without any trouble, she hesitated at the big wall but he coached her through and finished clear. He gave me a wink as he rode by us, I clapped and cheered out loud at his success, some of the others looked gloomy as they might have been thinking their chances were getting slim.

Everyone finished. Everyone said very little and the tension rose even more. There were no more jokes or wise cracks amongst friends; this is where it all became strictly business. Ted kept to himself and even Murt stopped cracking stupid comments. I thought 6.00pm would never come. We all sat in the formal living room, some people had made a cup of tea, some were pacing the floor and looking out the window. I just curled up on the sofa and twisted mums bracelet round and round. Then we could hear mumbling and footsteps approaching the room.

Finally in walked the Captain, who said something to a gentleman who was one of the selectors and shut the door firmly.

He looked around at each of us before talking; he looked at his list once more as if considering his selection and then took a deep breath.

"As you know, this is not easy" he looked around for a chair to sit on, Ted stood up and gave him his and made his way over to sit beside me on the sofa. "Thank you Ted" he continued. "As you know, this was extremely hard, the standard has never been as high and I congratulate those who have joined us here for the past few days. You are without a doubt, the cream of the country when it comes to Show Jumping. And for those of you who will not be making it any further, please do not be disappointed, there will be more opportunities and plenty more team events throughout the year." He cleared his throat and unfolded the piece of paper. It was now looking like a page that had been torn from 'The Book of Kells' to me.

"Let's make this simple… the names I call out, are the people and horse combinations that will be going to the Olympics." He looked around once more and began.

"Ted, congratulations" Beside me Ted gasped and put his hands in his head and turned to me, I gave him a hug but was anxious to know who was next...

"Murt, congratulations"

"Jesus Christ Captain, are you serious?" asked Murt questioning the Captain.

"Yes Murt, I am serious, but you are warned, you must be on your best behavior... no drinking..." Murt nodded. "No girls..."

"My wife will agree with you on that one Captain" said Murt smiling wide from cheek to cheek, everyone in the room gave a light laugh, but those of us without the name call where still sitting stiffly.

"And carrying on.... Padraig, congratulations" said the Captain. Padraig was an elderly man who had been to the Olympics many times, so this was nothing new to him. He nodded with gratitude.

"Two more places.... And this was the most difficult one." He looked at me and then turned his head and said "Jessica, your in." She clapped her hands together in excitement and looked around the room for everyone else to congratulate her, she only got nods and then it was down to me and the others in the room. Patrica, a fat lady from North of Ireland gave me evil eyes as she was thinking am I going to snatch her place. I suddenly felt like I shouldn't be there, everyone here had been riding since they were in nappies and I only started just over a year ago. Dads voice came into my head, the first time he spoke to Ted Walsh, he had said he thought I had something special… well let's see dad, let's see.

"And last but not least" said the Captain, stalling for a few seconds and then looked straight at me "Molly" and gave the first smile he had ever given all week. I sat there as the name took a few seconds to sink in, Ted stretched over and gave me a huge hug and rocked me back and forward, tears started to roll down my cheek and a lump formed in my throat, I couldn't speak, I was crying so much I couldn't even say thank you to anyone.

"Everyone else, well done. You are all free to go home today. Olympians… I want you all back here in two weeks' time. Thank you" and with that he left us all in the room. Everyone was talking, crying and laughing. Some crying because they were not picked. Patrica the fat lady walked over and stood in front of the sofa, I was a little scared incase she was going to lean down and punch me on the face, instead she leaned down and kissed my cheek.

"You're the one to watch sunshine, well done" she whispered in my ear. I thanked her as I watched her leave, her hopes had been flushed away I thought.

"Come here you" Ted said again and for the millionth time, gave me a kiss on the cheek and a huge hug. "We need to ring your mum and dad" he said pulling me up. And we ran towards a phone, just as he picked up the receiver and asked me for the number I took the phone from him and hung it back up.

"Look I'm sorry Ted, there's something I haven't told you" I needed to tell him about mum, I hadn't been truthful and I may as well tell him.

"What's up" he said curiously.

"My mum" I began "She died" He looked shocked and sorrowful as he put his arms around me once more. "I'm Ok, I'm Ok" I said honestly. "She died just after Christmas last year, she was on a bus when it crashed, and she was the only one who didn't survive."

"Oh Molly my darling, I'm so sorry, you

poor pet. And there's me asking where your mum was? I had no idea" He said still holding me tight. It felt really nice and comforting. Then as if to cheer me up, he lifted the phone and said "Will we tell him?"

Tears, laughter, screaming and a celebration in my dad's pub later, did it only sink in what was happening. There were so many forms and documents to be completed, fittings for uniforms, tons of team wear arrived and Shamrocks got loads of new rugs and strict instructions not be let run free through the Olympic Village! We travelled several times to the Sheikhs yard for training and the tension was growing. Jessica was featured on the six o'clock news as the new rising star and they even filmed her at home, all the publicity I got was my name on a list scrolling by as her interview took place. It was good enough for me. The cost of all the travelling and everything we needed to get to prepare was taking its toll on my dad. He didn't know I knew this, but he had taken out a loan with the credit union to fund our trips. The pub had become very quiet and I feared that when the Olympics were all over dad would have to sell and maybe start something else, or get a job. Whatever would happen at least we had both found each other and had become a little family. Mum was no longer with us in flesh but in spirit I could feel her beside me all the time.

Chapter 18

Dad, Kerry, Shamrocks and I travelled over on the ferry from Dublin to Holyhead and drove our rickety old truck to London. We had a problem at Dublin port where we were nearly not being allowed on the boat. Our truck, let me explain, is not really what you could describe as a luxury hotel on wheels. In fact it was Bills cow truck he used to take cattle to the market. We had painted it green and put in blow up beds and a curtain area to get changed behind. We had a portable loo and used a bottle of water and a bucket to wash our teeth, boil some water over a stove if we needed warm water. It wasn't pretty or luxury but at least it was to be our home for the next two weeks. But at the port after my dad re-started the engine to go onto the boat, a huge cloud of black smoke filled the car park. People complained as they tried to roll up their windows as fast as they could. A couple in a flashy red convertible car shouted and swore "What is that heap of crock?" or we got "You're polluting the environment" or "Piece of shit" it got worse really and the guy directing cars and trucks onto the boat put a scarf over his face as he coughed and coughed, he told dad not to start the banger until all other cars had disembarked at Holyhead... dad agreed but obviously didn't take any notice as we were the first to get off the boat the other side, leaving the car deck in a thick black cloud, we even heard someone shout "FIRE"!

All the equestrian events were being held at "Greenwich Park" and upon arrival I could not believe my eyes for the sea of crowds, horses, groom, screaming children, stewards and organisers franticly handing out passes and schedules. All the Irish equestrian team had their own block of stables, our own cooling down area which consisted of jets of water pumped from overhead to cool down horses and riders. The heat was much more humid than Clada, I thought London would be the same but it wasn't, it was as hot as Florida had been. It made my dad sweat and Kerry told him off for eating hot dogs and fries all the time. Shamrocks had a stable next to Teds bay mare that didn't seem to want to know Shamrocks despite his advances. She would squeal and raise her tail up high and prance over to the other side of her stable. "Just like her owner" I said to Shamrocks as I watched Ted flirt with an American rider. Her name was Betty Bootley and she was tall, slim, blonde and had the biggest horse truck I had ever seen in my life. Unfortunately for us when we arrived we were told to park next to her truck. It made our old wooden green truck look like the Beverly Hillbillies car. Her truck was huge, sprayed with the American flag all over and her name plastered on every available space along with her sponsorship logos of Coca-Cola, Mercedes and SKY TV. We didn't get off to a good start with our new neighbour. Upon arrival her dad, a fat American man with sleek black hair that looked like a hair piece screamed and shouted at my dad for the pollution that had just come in through his windows.

"God Dam Irish" he shouted walking away.

Kerry smirked and put two fingers up behind his back. "God dam Yank" she shouted after him and as he turned around she looked away in case he would return and say something to her.

"OK, let's just keep to ourselves. Luckily we don't have to start this truck until we leave" said dad relieved.

"Do you think we'll have a medal on the dash board when we leave?" I asked him smiling.

"Well Molly my darling... Who would have thought you could ride? And who would have thought that Shamrocks was not the crazy horse after all? And who in their wildest dreams would have thought that we made it to the Olympics?" He smiled and looked so proud of me. "I think, anything is possible!"

"I'm going to cry" said Kerry as she gave me a hug. Dad gave a big sigh and looked at her.

"Ohh will you shtop" he said "You're such a softy, and I'm sorry to throw this at you, but do you think maybe this time you could actually be a bit of a groom?" He raised one eyebrow and looked at her for a response.

"Don't be stupid Martin, I'm terrified of horses" she said with a smile towards me.

"Then why did you come?" he was trying to sound serious but I secretly knew the reason and I think deep down so did Kerry.

"Because you invited me" She said abruptly "anyway, I'm Molly's friend". We both smiled and I gave my dad a nod.

"That's right" I said in a very west of Ireland accent.

"Right let's get sorted and ready for tonight's opening ceremony" said dad hopping out of the truck.

"Oh, I'm so proud of you Molly" said Kerry

again hugging me once more and starting to cry again. It was going to be a very long two weeks I decided.

It was surreal. I was part of one of the biggest events in history. Shamrocks name and my name would be encrypted forever as one of the millions who took part in the Olympic Games. I felt scared and alone, even though Ted was in the Irish squad and getting ready to do our lap around the giant stadium, I felt he was more interested in finding out where the American team were. He looked clearly smitten and I felt like a child once more. As I talked to other members of various disciplines, none of them knew who I was or seemed to care too much. They all had video camcorders and other devices to record their memories, I heard out loud over the PA system that flooded the stadium "IRELAND" and everyone around me cheered and waved Irish flags as they ran out into the madness. It was crazy, you couldn't even hear yourself think. Lights flashed from every direction all around us. There were millions of people and even though with so many people, I was the loneliest person in the world. I tried to find dad and Kerry but had no idea where they would be. I wished I could have brought Shamrocks too.

"Come on Molly" said Ted who suddenly appeared beside me "This is it, all the hard work" he waved his hands in the air as if he had won a prize. I nodded and smiled but to me, this was not what it was all about, this was just the beginning and I was not long there until I felt like I needed to leave. I looked around to see where I could go, but I couldn't see an exit, dancers and fireworks were about to go off in the middle of the stadium. I began to panic and I looked for a way out through the crowed. It was hopeless. People pushed and shoved, other members of the squad said "What's your problem?" or "Where do you think you're going?" Someone even grabbed me by the scruff of my neck and tried to pull me backwards. I let out a cry of "HELP" but nobody seemed to care, they just marched forward and pushed me even more. I broke away as I could hear Ted shouting "Molly, Molly what's wrong?" I just needed to get away. Finally a space in the crowd, I tried to run up the outside looking for a way out, the silly heeled shoes we were made to wear began to hurt my feet so I stopped and took them off. I threw them to a little girl in the audience and lifted my skirt and began to run.

I didn't really know where I was running to, but I needed to get out of there. Flashes got closer to my face and some guys with cameras were now running after me, some in front with a microphone in my face asking "what's your name?" I wiped tears away from my eyes and ran as fast as I could which felt like a full loop of the arena before I saw the exit, I ran and ran and ran all the way until the buzzing of the noise was behind me. My feet were sore and I had cuts on my soles but I didn't care. I hoped nobody noticed that I had escaped. I waved at a black taxi and asked him to take me to Greenwich Park. When I got there I had to walk to the other end of the show grounds and right down to where our truck was parked. The show grounds were extremely quiet because everyone was at the opening ceremony. I quickly got into our truck and turned on the torch as we had no lights. I examined my bare feet and dabbed them with water from the bucket. They were skinned and bleeding. I looked around for plasters but could only see some bandages that belonged to Shamrocks. I wrapped my feet up best I could and pulled on a pair of jeans and a t-shirt. My trainers would not fit over my feet so I put on my bunny slippers and hobbled towards Shamrocks stable.

How does he know? I ask myself every time. Before I even see him, he whinnies and kicks his door with excitement that I am here. As I got closer he rubbed his nostrils against my hair. I went into his stable and sat down beside him. My feet were so sore but at least I felt happy. He lowered his big long face in front of me to stroke. I told him about the flashing lights and how afraid I was of all those people. He gave light husky whinny's as I spoke as if acknowledging what I was going through. Then he circled the stable and slowly bent his left knee and then his right before collapsing down on his soft clean bed of shavings. He gave out a big sigh and I crawled over to his big muscular neck and stroked it. He was so beautiful and he had put all his trust in me. How vulnerable he was and yet how brave, all together. I lowered my head and rested it on his neck, he didn't seem to mind, so I curled up my knees and got comfortable and I felt him breathe in and out, the movement made me feel relaxed and sleepy, so I closed my eyes for a few minutes. Just to feel safe and not alone.

Chapter 19

"Blap.... Blap" is what I heard as I stiffly opened my eyes and turned my head. I had Shamrocks hair from his neck prickly sticking to the side of my cheek. I sat up and rubbed my arm, it was freezing cold. I looked towards the stable door and with that I had to cover my eyes quickly as another "Blap" went off and blinded my vision. Shamrocks nudged me to move as he scrambled to his feet while I tried to figure out what was happening. Then I heard an English speaking gentleman shout "She's here, down here mate, I got a few pictures. This was so easy mate" Who the hell was that? And why was he taking photos of me asleep? As the man turned and was shouting at his fellow mate, Shamrocks ran to the stable door and with his nose pushed the man and still holding his camera straight onto the ground where he tried to clumsily get up shouting "easy boy, nice pony.... Don't hurt me..." I looked over the stable door and stared at the man on the floor. He was geeky looking with glasses and a check shirt and khaki coloured pants. He reminded me of Clarke Kent from Superman.

"What the hell are you doing?" I asked him "You're scaring my horse for a start. Are you some kind of dodgy stalker or something? because if you are, Shamrocks here is very protective and he'll easily break your nose and accidently kick you in the you know where!"

"Jesus, stop it, no, no please… don't let him out, I beg you miss, please" he was petrified poor idiot. But what the hell was he doing? If dad saw him he would definitely give him a punch. "Please, I'll leave you alone if you just promise not to let that beast out" he said.

"OK, OK you big softy, I won't open the door until you leave" I promised as I watched him brush off the dirt from his bottom.

"That's Molly, you're a star" he said as he walked away.

Hang on a second I thought. How did he know who I was? "Hey you" I shouted after him "How do you know who I am?"

"It's all over the paper and television. You're like a fugitive, every ones been looking for the Irish girl who made headlines last night" he said looking back. What was he talking about?

"Come back" I shouted as he ran down the stable aisles.

"You promised not to open that door till I left" He screamed back, and he ran out into the open yard.

"What's that all about?" I asked Shamrocks. "Anyway time for your breakfast, I'll go get it, you wait here and don't go killing anyone else" and I took his empty bucket from the night before to head towards our truck to fill it up with feed.

As soon as I walked out of the stable aisle a swarm of cameras ran around my face and microphones were being shoved under my nose.

"Molly, why did you run away?" I heard a voice ask. And another "Do you feel being at the Olympics is too much pressure?" and another one asked "Are you a delinquent child? Do you run away all the time?"

What the hell was going on? I looked straight into the face of a television camera and microphones were still being pushed into my face. Where was dad? I needed help. I pushed by everyone and ran as fast as I could in my bunny slippers, my feet still killing me towards our little truck. Luckily they could not get by security at this point and they stayed at the gate shouting after me.

Once I reached our truck I was so grateful and so happy when the door swung open and I saw my dad. He looked at me and gave a little cry.

"Where have you been?" He demanded. "The police are looking for you right now, what happened out there?"

"I don't know what's going on!" I shouted to him.

"Molly, you can't just run away from something like this. Do you want to back out? Because the Captain has been on and frankly he's a little concerned about your mental state, and so am I!"

"Martin stop it" said Kerry who had swollen mascara streaked eyes.

"No, I need to know. Why did you run away? What other people wouldn't give to have a chance like this, what's wrong with you?"

"What's wrong with me?" I sobbed "there's nothing *wrong* with me dad" I started to cry and then he came closer to me to hold me tight.

"shhhh shhhhh" he put his warm arms around my cold arms and stroked my hair. "Molly, has anyone hurt you?"

"No" I choked.

"Anyone said anything nasty?" he asked.

"No, nothing." I swallowed a huge lump of saliva that was forming in my mouth "I just felt" I couldn't bring myself to speak. Dad stroked my cheek and wiped away some tears. "I just felt all alone" I burst out crying again.

"You're not alone, you have me" he held my shoulders and gave them a shake.

"Don't leave me on my own anymore" I asked him.

"I won't I promise" he said leaning down and kissing the top of my head.

"You have me too sweetheart" said Kerry embarrassing us both. "And I love you with all my heart" she said honestly.

I saw dad and her looking into each other's eyes when there was a loud knock on the door that made us all jump a mile. Dad walked over and answered it.

"Irish, first you pollute our space, now you got paparazzi harassing my Betty wanting to know everything about your daughter. Sort it out Irish before I put in an official complaint!" said the fat yank from next door. Dad looked at him, smiled and then said at the top of his voice;

"Top of the morning to ya", and shut the door. We all started to laugh and I explained what had happened with the cameras and microphones.

"Don't you worry, you leave all that to me" said dad. "I'm off to see the Captain and tell him all is ok. You get a sleep and Kerry maybe you could give Shamrocks his breakfast?"

"What?" she asked "This is outrageous! Do you not realise that my nails have been specially painted for this event" and she showed my dad her beautiful painted finger nails each had a little Irish flag on them.

"Fabulous" said dad scooping feed into the bucket "Now, give this to the donkey and then get some decent breakfast for us all" and off he went.

"What did his last slave die of?" she said as soon as he went out of sight. Then she looked over at me "Oh honey, I didn't mean that, I'm so sorry, are you OK?"

I laughed at her joke and at how apologetic she was.

She went with Shamrocks feed wearing a huge sombrero and dark glasses to avoid the "paps" as she put it. This was right up her street I thought!

A few hours later I woke up to find dad, Kerry and the Captain all sat on stools outside the truck talking, waiting for me to wake up. I opened the door as they were discussing the 1000m mens relay that had just occurred. Kerry was lying on one of Shamrocks new rugs on the ground sunbathing with a tiny pink bikini on. The captain and dad didn't seem to mind at all!

"Here she is, the runaway jockey" said the Captain sternly as he got to his feet.

"I'm sorry Captain" I said apologetically. "I just panicked, I am so sorry"

"The person who never made a mistake, never made anything" he said and gestured for me to sit down. "Are you alright now?"

"Yes, I'm fine thanks" I said taking a can of coke from my dad. "Am I dropped?" I asked him. I needed to know, if I was then there was nothing else I could do.

"No, no, no, no" said Captain "You worry too much. I'm here because unfortunately the press have picked up on your little escape, and they even interviewed some members of the community in Clada where you are from... A Mrs Hegarty has stated on national TV that your horse has rampaged through her shop several times and stolen polo mints" he raised his eyebrows "and they have also dug up your past. Saying you're from a rough part of Dublin, probably took drugs, your mother was a prostitute and killed herself and finally the best one I heard yet... was that you stole Shamrocks!" he laughed and looked at my dad. It was all lies. Why and who would make up suck stories?

"Well, it's all not true.... How can we set the record straight?" I asked.

"For now, we do nothing. If anything, its publicity, and that can be an advantage sometimes. It means people now feel they have you to watch. Not you watching them." He stood up and looked at Kerry baking in the sun.

"Thanks Captain" said my dad shaking his hand.

"Molly, I want you fit and well. Tomorrow I will meet you at 5.30am in the bottom schooling ring, don't tell anyone, just be there ok." And the captain nodded and departed.

"What about the paparazzi?" I asked "and all

those lies?"

"Don't worry about them, you leave them to me" said dad "I'm off to have a look around, Molly you better stay low for today OK".

"OK" I said.

Kerry turned to me "Finally, some girl time. Get into your shorts and come lie with me and we'll talk boys" I giggled at her, I loved her girly way, I was so unfeminine these days from living with dad, so I was perfectly happy to stay and relax with her for a while.

"So what's up with Ted?" asked Kerry straight to the chase.

"I don't know?" I said honestly "one minute he's my best friend and I have butterflies in my tummy, then the next he's flirting with Miss USA and making my blood boil!"

"Ok, so horses I know nothing about" said Kerry sitting up and pushing her sunglasses above her head.

"That makes two of us Kerry!" I joked.

"But men… I know!" she said. She took a sip of her diet coke and continued. "If you want a man to notice you, you have to play it cool and hard to get. For instance, when you see Ted, don't just run up and say 'Hi Ted it's me Molly, how are you?' understand?"

"Yeah, but that's only being polite as a friend would do" I said.

"Yes, but you don't want to get into the whole best buddy thing, then he'll never think about you in another way" said Kerry.

"So what do I do?" I asked.

"Next time you see him, you act like you don't notice him, or that you don't care about him. This will intrigue him, make him jealous. He will want to know why you're ignoring him. And you have to have, a pretend boyfriend. This will make him mad jealous!" said Kerry as she took out her sun lotion to rub onto my shoulders.

"So I lie to him is what you're saying?" I asked.

"Yes well done Molly, you are a quick learner" she looked proud that I understood her mad method. I had nothing to lose, so I was going to give it a try.

"And, why don't we do a makeover, nothing

drastic. Tomorrow night.. Pending on how you jump, let me transform you into a swan!" she pleaded.

"Are you saying I'm ugly?" I asked shocked and turned to face her.

"Oh no sweetheart, you're so beautiful, you don't need me to transform you… just maybe make you look a little more flirty… for Ted???" she asked.

"Ok, but don't tell dad or he'll go mad" I exclaimed.

"Leave your father to me, I can handle him" she said lying back down to sun bath some more.

"So why aren't you in love?" I asked her.

"I'm happy for now" she said "but maybe someday I'll fall head over heels" I thought her face looked a little bit sad, so I changed the subject quick.

"So what could I wear tomorrow night?" I asked her "all I have is team wear"

"I got plenty of stuff, we will rock the show ground tomorrow night" she smiled at me as I lay down beside her.

"You miss your momma honey?" she asked.

I went silent for a little thinking about mum and the similar talks we would have, I nodded at her and said "I think she brought me to you more than dad!" this made her laugh and we both had a hug before resting our limbs in the hot sun.

Chapter 20

It was 5.30am and Dad and I had Shamrocks already warmed up. The Captain gave shamrocks and I a light schooling and a few easy jumps, he explained how the course was to look that afternoon, told me not to be nervous. Not to be nervous.. Oh no, why should I be? I am the youngest rider in the competition, the whole world thinks I'm a nutcase and that my deceased mother was a prostitute and that Shamrocks is wild and I had stolen him.

"No pressure!" I replied to him trying not to let him know what I was thinking in my head.

As we returned to the yard Jessica queried where we had been and got into a tantrum when she heard I had a session one to one with the Captain.

"Why the hell does she get the Royal treatment, suppose you need it darling, considering your upbringing and all…" she said sarcastically trying to raise my temper.

"Shut up Walsh" said Ted who was busy getting his mare tacked up.

"And what is it to you anyway?" said Jessica

to Ted "I'd watch out Molly, I don't think you're flavour of the month any more... He seems to like the taste of American grill" she said swinging her whip around in circles walking towards Teds stable. "Isn't that right Ted?"

"I've told you once, don't make me tell you again" said Ted. "And stop swinging your whip around, it makes my horse jumpy".

"Oh but Ted, once upon a time you would not have said such a thing about my whip" she giggled at her own amusement. "So Molly, did he do you and dump you too?"

"Shut up you stupid cow" shouted Ted. "Don't mind her Molly".

"Don't worry, I won't" I said from the stable next to them.

"That's because you're a lady" said Ted as he walked over to the side of his stable "fancy lunch with me later?"

"Sorry, no can do Ted. I'm having lunch with my boyfriend" I turned away and bit my lip. Shit, what have I said? This was complete and utter lies.

"Who, who's that then?" stammered Ted

who was staring over the partition wanting an answer.

"Err, you don't know him, he's a guy" I answered.

"Well I presumed that if he's your boyfriend, he would be a guy" he demanded.

"Yeah funny! You'll meet him tonight, at the ball" I said still not facing him for fear he would see me lie.

"What's his name?" asked Ted.

"His name, his name is errr...." And I really tried to think quickly but all I came out with was "Ollie Pix" I think I was thinking of the photographer that took out photo yesterday morning.

"Ollie Pix?" said Ted "That has to be the weirdest name I had ever heard. "What does he do?"

"He's a photographer" I said still not facing him.

"Ollie Pix, the photographer?" he questioned.

"Yep that's his name, my boyfriend" I lied once more. "You'll see him tomorrow".

"Oh that's sweet, are you allowed out after the dark?" said Jessica in her usual bitchy tone. "Of course you are, silly me, you even stay out all night and have the metropolitan police search all London for you, how I forget these things" she said still swinging her whip around "In fact, maybe you were looking for a corner to do your business from, just like your mother!"

"Right that's it Walsh, FECK OFF" said Ted as he opened his stable door and grabbed her wrist. "Don't you ever speak to her like that again or I'll feckin use this whip the same way as you treat your animals!"

"LET ME GO" she screamed but nobody around seemed to care. Murt was walking towards the stables and saw the commotion and pulled Ted off Jessica.

"Do you want us to get banned from competing?" asked Murt who looked at the two in disgrace.

"I'm going for a ride" said Ted as he pulled his mare out of her stable and mounted her right in front of everyone and trotted down the aisle with people having to jump out of his way fast or else he would have hit them.

Luckily dad or Kerry hadn't heard what went on, and so I tried to put what Jessica had said behind me the best I could. I tried to focus on the day's events ahead.

There were to be over one hundred competitors in the qualifier and the top fifty were to qualify for the final in two days' time. As I walked the course with my dad we went over every possible trick that could be laid out. The captain walked it with us also so I was sure what to do. The jumps were higher than I had ever seen, wider than me lying down, and the water jump was literally a swimming pool. I knew Shamrocks was not a spooky horse but he was only 15.2hh and these jumps were bigger than him. I was scared and felt over faced. Had this opportunity been too much? I was so excited to get here, but now that I was here, quite frankly, I was petrified. All along I thought it would be no problem, I slept well, ate well and now I suddenly felt extremely sick.

After walking the course several times I ran towards the riders toilets. I did not care who else was there. I had no time to be a lady. I closed the bathroom door and knelt down over the toilet bowl. It needed no help, my breakfast and lunch came rising up my throat like cement. I groaned as I threw up, there seemed to be more towards the end but nothing was coming up. I washed my face and hands before checking my reflection in the mirror. I looked horrendous, I was pale, my eyes were streaming and my neat long red hair was escaping through the bun that was trying to keep it in place. I decided to take out the bun and instead tied my hair in a ponytail and let it fall down my back. Just then Kerry ran in to the toilets.

"Molly sweetheart, you don't have time to be sick. Come on now" and she grabbed my hand and lead me out of the toilets and we ran all the way to the collecting ring where dad was walking Shamrocks around.

Shamrocks looked stunning. He never shined as much in his life. As I mounted him my dad produced from his inside pocket a clover leafed shamrock and pinned it onto my green riding jacket.

"This was sent over from your Aunt Anne" he said "It grew on your mum's grave".

I felt overwhelmed. It was the best thing I had been given. My mum was with me. I smiled at dad and turned to walk Shamrocks towards the busy collecting arena when I suddenly turned back to him and shouted out loudly "I love you dad".

"Molly get a move on" shouted the captain. I

had to focus now, no more prep, this was it. I had to get my act together and I had to do it quick. I approached a few jumps a little off and the Captain swore at me a few times and told me what I was doing wrong. I tried to concentrate more and then as if running out of time to live I heard our names be announced as next to go.

I walked over to the arena entrance calmly. Dad, Kerry and the Captain all wished us luck. I blessed myself as we entered into the arena. Yet again, it was like entering a world where nobody else existed, a lonely place. But I had Shamrocks and I had my mum.

"So, the first rider to go for Ireland" announced the commentator "Is Molly O'Neil riding the little Irish grey, Shamrocks"

The bell went signaling for us to start. I kicked him into a medium to fast pace canter and approached the first jump.

Chapter 21

The crowd roared, I looked behind us in astonishment. I looked up at the score board, and then I searched the sea of faces for dad or Kerry. I didn't slow down; I didn't even hear what the commentator was saying. Was this really happening? I exited the arena at full speed, nearly knocking over a Spanish groom. I kept going until we reached the other end of the arena. I turned Shamrocks who was breathing heavily and sweating and steaming like a train. Through the crowd I saw my dad running as fast as he could towards us. I jumped off Shamrocks and ran with my arms open to my dad, my feet were still sore but I didn't care. He picked me up and swung me around in circles.

"You did it! You went clear; it means you're guaranteed a place in the final!" He had tears rolling down his face with joy. Kerry came running behind to celebrate too.

"We have a place in the final!" I corrected him.

I couldn't believe it, a clear round. Everyone gathered around to congratulate me, the TV cameras and microphones were in our faces.

"There's been a lot of rumours going around about your past, what do you have to say about that?" asked a journalist.

"Don't believe what you read in the papers" I said and we pushed by the heaving crowd who all wanted to get a piece of the little grey from Ireland.

As I sat in Shamrocks stable watching him munch through another carrot I couldn't help feel excited. We had come all this way and I had overheard the American girl Betty say that "the redhead Irish was the one to watch in the final!" Dad was so thrilled that he went to the beer tent to celebrate and was beginning to sing some Irish songs the last time I checked on him. Kerry had gone for a shower and told me to meet her at 7.00pm sharp! I gave Shamrocks a big hug and a kiss goodnight and told him I would check on him on our way back from the ball and made him promise not to laugh because I was going to be wearing a dress!

9.00pm and dad knocked on the truck door to find out where his two best girls were.

"We're nearly finished" shouted Kerry.

"I left you at 3.30 Kerry, what the hell are you doing? Molly, you'll be ready, come on out and we'll go on ahead" said dad.

"I'm nearly ready too, you go on back in dad and we'll be there soon" I shouted back to him.

"Ok, ok... women!" it was something he said a lot I thought.

"Are you sure about this Kerry?" I asked. I couldn't really see how I looked. We were now using a torch and a small mirror to try and look at ourselves. Kerry was wearing an elegant long red dress with one strap. Her blond hair was let out loose and I thought she looked like a beautiful princess. She had given me to wear a shiny beaded strapless gold dress and gold high heels. It was mid length and showed off my tanned legs from the day before. Kerry had put rollers in my hair then pinned it up slightly. She did my makeup and even told me to spray perfume between my legs... she was definitely going OTT I thought.

We wobbled along the grass and chipped paths towards the large marquee. Many people were there and lots of people congratulated us on my round and wanted to know more about Shamrocks. I tried to find dad but couldn't see him for the crowd. I got Kerry a glass of champagne and an orange juice for myself. As we mingled amongst the rich and famous I noticed Sheikh Mombassa who raised a glass towards me and signaled for us to join him.

"Kerry, I want you to meet a friend of mine" I said to her as she followed me smiling towards the group of people. Only when we got closer did she realise who she was to meet.

"Hello, how are you?" I asked the Sheikh as he leaned forward to kiss me on both cheeks.

"Very well Miss Molly. I am so happy to have watched you today. I have high hopes for you and your little grey wonder" he said in his Arabic broken English.

"This is my friend Kerry" I introduced them. "Kerry this is Sheikh Mombassa"

For some reason Kerry felt completely out of place as she bowed and said in an English accent "How do you do?" Why was she talking funny?

The Sheikh took her hand and kissed it "It is a pleasure. Are you enjoying the Games?"

"Yes it is truly delightful" answered Kerry. Oh dear God I thought, what is she doing? "We were only talking about the miraculous history that will be set by one self at these Games, isn't that correct Molly?" she looked at me in what I can only describe as... her posh look!

"Yes, that's right" I answered her in my west of Ireland accent. Her smile went to a frown quickly. "I am looking for my dad, so if you will excuse me, I hope to meet you again soon."

"We will meet again, and good luck in the final. Kerry it was a pleasure" said the Sheikh kissing her hand again.

"The pleasure is all mine" she said as I dragged her away into the crowd.

I spotted my dad at the end of the bar with Murt and Padraig. Murt had not qualified; he was the only Irish not too. He was in fact totally and utterly intoxicated and was singing an old Irish ballad. My dad turned and faced us both as we approached him.

"Molly, what happened to you?" he said studying me up and down "You look beautiful, not sure if I fully approve but you look gorgeous. Just stay close to me tonight, I know what these Show Jumping fellas are after!" then he asked "Where's Kerry?"

As if the room had parted into two my dad's mouth dropped to the floor, his pint of Guinness tilted and was spilling slowly to the ground. He looked at Kerry like I had never seen before. Bingo I thought!

"Is that…Is that Perry?" asked a pissed Murt.

"Kerry" I shouted at him. He was so numb and I don't know how his poor wife put up with him.

"Martin" said Kerry back to her casual voice again all of a sudden. "Want to buy me a drink" she held his hand and straightened his glass so it wasn't spilling anymore. My dad stayed staring and in a voice I had not heard before, that was extremely high and made him sound like a little boy he asked;

"What would you like?" then he cleared his throat and asked again in a more deeply manly voice.

"Pint of the good stuff please Mr O'Neil" she said.

"It's awful" said dad finishing his pint. "Worst pint I have ever had"

"And the one before that one, was that as

bad?" asked Kerry.

"Worse" he said. Then he stretched over to the bar tender and asked him for a bottle of champagne.

"You trying to impress me Mr O'Neil?" she asked, actually looking impressed too!

"Might be" said my dad, He poured two glasses of champagne, spilling most of it onto the floor and missing the flutes. He then drunkenly lifted his glass into the air "let's raise a toast, to my little girl here, for taking us all too where we are right now"

"Here, here" said a few people around us.

"And to the lovely, Kerry" He looked at Kerry straight in the eyes. This is it. He's going to propose. "To the lovely Kerry who drives us all mad, but keeps us all going" and we all looked at dad to see what he was going to say next "and to the one woman who I want to spend.." he sat on his stool and took another long drink, looked at everyone sleepily and just lowered his head and began to snore.

"Dad" I gave him a shake and he opened his eyes "Molly darling, well done today" and closed his eyes again, nearly falling off the stool but luckily was caught by Ted who suddenly appeared form nowhere.

"Let's get you home Mr O'Neil" said Ted who lifted one side of him and Kerry quickly lifted the other. What a night I thought, first it takes us hours to get ready and now we have to leave because dad is so drunk. We struggled getting him into the truck and into the blow up bed. I took off his shoes and covered him up.

"He'll be fine Kerry, let's go back" I said to her.

"No honey, you go. I'm not really in the mood now" she said.

"I'm not going back on my own" I said to her.

"I'll watch her" said Ted.

"I'm not some lost dog Ted, I don't want to go back" I said.

"Molly, you look so fabulous, go enjoy yourself, Ted have her back by midnight before she turns back into her old clothes!" she laughed.

"I like her in her old clothes" said Ted who

was talking very cautiously. Kerry smiled and reassured me she would rather just change into her pajamas and read some of her book with the torch. Maybe she was hoping dad would wake up, but if I knew dad, he was going to be asleep for a long, long time.

As we arrived back at the ball Ted asked me where Ollie Pix was? I had totally forgotten my lie and looking into his eyes I think it said it all.

"You had me convinced" he said laughing "Why did you lie?"

"I dunno, maybe to piss Jessica off, or maybe even you?" I said bravely. We looked over and saw Jessica being chatted up again by Murt. "She has no shame" I continued "She knows he's married right?"

"Yep. And he has children. Guys like that make me sick" said Ted as he waited at the bar to be served. "Want anything?"

"Just a coke please" I answered. I looked around for Betty Bootley and dared to ask but thought I should "So where's Betty tonight?"

"Well, on a plane back home as far as I know" he said. Is this why he's back talking to me I thought?

"Why?" I asked.

"Turns out her horse was tested, and he had a trace of drugs, so her dad put her on the first flight out of here" he told me.

"Too bad" I said sarcastically rubbing his arm.

"I like you O'Neil, but you're only sixteen and I'm not sure you're ready for a boyfriend, so I keep my distance from time to time" said Ted. At least he didn't dislike me I thought.

"I'm old enough to make my own decisions" I said. I wasn't quite sure how this was going, I like him, he likes me. I'm new to this, he's not. What's the answer?... Oh where's Kerry when I need her?

"Tell you what, when the Games are over. Win or lose, I'll come to Clada and take you out on a proper date. Deal?" he asked.

"What? like, a kissing sort of date" I teased.

"Yeah, maybe" He said.

"What if we both kiss and it turns out to be a mistake, shame for you to drive all the way to Clada to find out" I knew I was suddenly beginning to be flirty.

"You're worth the trip" he said smiling all the time.

"Tell you what, I win gold I get to kiss you" I said.

"And I win gold, I get to kiss that little hottie over there" he said as I looked through the crowd looking to see who he was talking about. "I'm pulling your leg!"

"Ha ha" I said sarcastically. Not really knowing a lot of people and I knew Ted was anxious to talk to some of his friends I said good night to him and made my way back to the truck. Just as I was getting closer I heard Ted behind me.

"You forgot this" he said. I turned in the darkly lit area of the camp ground to see what he was holding.

"What did I forget?" I asked him. He then pulled me towards his warm body and slowly pressed his lips onto mine. His tongue slid slowly into my mouth which made me want to faint a little. His hands went through my long red wavy hair as he touched the back of my neck. When we stopped I was swaying around a little and felt weak.

"Good night" he said and turned back towards the party. "Oh, and I definitely want that date!" he shouted over his shoulder. I didn't even answer him properly, I was still feeling weak and trying to get my head around what had happened before he was out of sight.

"Good night Ted" I whispered. I jumped up high in excitement and did a little victory dance; then I remembered promising Shamrocks I would say good night to him, so I headed in the direction of the stables to confide in my best friend.

Chapter 22

That's weird, I thought. Shamrocks always knows when I'm approaching him unless the high heels are putting him off. As I walked crookedly down the stable aisle I could hear the resting of other horses, champions were within this barn and our little wonder boy was one of them. Horses munched on their hay nets and some looked out to nosy who I was. Shamrocks head did not appear out; perhaps today's course took more out of him than we had thought. As I approached I could hear grunts and groans, "urrrrggghhhh". It didn't sound like his usual sleeping sound. As I got closer I peered over the door and found Shamrocks stretched pout flat. His mouth was slightly open, his ears were lifeless, his eyes open and his huge body gave another large grunt. He looked like a beached whale.

I quickly opened the door and ran to his side, I rubbed his neck, it felt sweaty and clammy. I rubbed his face and he tried to move his eyes towards me. What was happening to him? Why was he so sick? I needed to get help, quickly. I felt a lump form in my throat and I felt my eyes fill with sorrow. I loved this horse so much, please God don't let him die.

"You stay right there honey, I'm just going to get some help" I leaned over and gave him a big long kiss on his cheek; he guzzled a noise through his nostrils. I got a rug and laid it over his body, I didn't know if he was hot or cold, I left the stable door wide open and took of my stupid heels and ran as fast as I had ever run in my life. Who would I get? Dad was unconscious and Kerry knew nothing about horses, so I ran straight back to the marquee to find Ted. He was standing at the bar where we had stood earlier, this time he had a pretty blonde beside him and his hand on her back talking into her ear. I didn't care; I was more concerned about Shamrocks. I ran to his side and grabbed his arm.

"Where's the Captain? Or the team vet?" I asked sternly.

"Molly, I thought you had gone to bed" said Ted sheepily and looking at the pretty blonde who sipped her cocktail looking at my bare feet in disapproval.

"Well lucky I didn't, for more reasons than one! Now do you know where they are or NOT?" I demanded loudly which made a few people turn and stare.

"Captains over there" said Ted pointing within the crowd.

I turned on my tippy toes and ran to the captain's side and whispered in his ear about Shamrocks. He quickly put his drink down and ran towards the stable barn, ringing our team vet on the way. When we arrived back Shamrocks was still lying as I had left him. The Captain rubbed his neck and spoke softly to him. I began to shake and cry as I held his head. It wasn't long before the team vet came running down the yard, half-dressed he put his glasses on and asked some questions.

"When did you last leave him today?" he asked me.

"About 7.30, and then around twenty minutes ago I came to say good night to him" I sobbed.

"What did he have for his tea?" asked the vet.

"His usual, oats, nuts and a bottle of Guinness" I told him. The vet got up and walked over to Shamrocks feed bucket; he took a handful out and shook his head.

"Someone's trying to kill your horse" he said

bluntly.

"What do you mean?" I asked.

"In this bucket is dry sugar beet, it needs to be soaked to be consumed, but someone has given him the dry nuts which have swelled up inside his stomach. I'm afraid Molly you better prepare yourself for the worst. I'll do all I can but I can't guarantee anything".

I roared out crying and fell to Shamrocks head, I bent down and stroked his face, rubbing around his eyes and telling him that everything was going to be alright. Ted came to my side and tried to pull me away.

"Get off me" I snapped. "He's my horse and I am not leaving his side".

He nodded in respect and walked away. The vet got a long tube and lubricated it before pushing it under Shamrocks tail. He grunted more, it must have been hurting him. All the time the vet kept talking to him, reassuring him and trying to lift my spirits. He poured some substance into a funnel which was going into his stomach; he also got several injections in the neck. When the vet was finished he listened to his heart. He shook his head and looked at me.

"I've done all I can Molly. It's up to him now, please, why don't you find your dad?" said the vet.

I shook my head and told him that I wasn't leaving his side. The Captain was on the phone all the time and I heard him say to someone to 'get O'Neil down here asap'. It was starting to get light outside and grooms and riders were beginning to turn up for their day's events or training. Many people walked over to look in the stable. I never looked at anyone, but I could hear people say "She's still wearing her ball dress". I couldn't care a less about what I was still wearing or about that silly boy Ted, filling me with false hopes. All that mattered to me now was the one thing that saved me from falling apart when mum died, and now here he is, maybe at the end of his life too.

A little while later I heard my dad and Kerry running towards us. He took one look at me and shamrocks cuddled together, he put his hands on his head and fell to his knees beside us.

"Molly, I'm so sorry I wasn't here for you" he leaned over to give me a kiss on my head.

"It's not your fault dad" I said.

"We're going to find out who did this, I

promise you." He said. Truth was, what was done was done, I just didn't want him to die. He dies, I die, I thought.

Kerry stood in the doorway sobbing; she came over and put her hands around my shoulders.

"Why don't you come with me and we'll get you freshened up" said Kerry.

"That's a good idea" said my dad.

"NO" I said out loud, "I'm not leaving him , he needs me like I need him". Just then Shamrocks lifted his head slightly and back down again. His eyes began to blink a little. "Shamrocks, it's me" I told him, and again he tried to lift his head.

"CAPTAIN" shouted my dad to the captain who was on the phone. He came running in and called the vet. The vet arrived within minutes. He put a head collar on Shamrocks and a lead.

"OK, he's responding, this is good. Now we need to get him up and get him walking" said the vet.

"Why?" I asked.

"He has colic, we need to get him moving and fingers crossed, he has a pooh! Then we'll be out of the woods. OK Everyone I need your help, two over that side, two behind, two here and I'll pull his head" instructed the vet.

So with seven of us we managed to get him to his feet. He wanted to lie straight back down but we all lifted and pulled him out the doorway, out onto the aisle where everyone pushed things back to make a clear path for us to get him outside.

Outside I could not believe my eyes. For there at the railings looking on where loads of cameras, microphones and people chanting Shamrocks name. The story of the little grey from Ireland who was favorite to win gold got out that he had been poisoned and now fighting for his life.

"Come on Shamrocks" chanted some people at the side line, they were even wearing t-shirts saying 'Shamrocks for Gold'.

It took us a while but then eventually he decided to help himself and took a few steps by himself, and then he would fail and fall again. We all held him up and encouraged him to walk more. He took a few more steps again, and then suddenly he put all his weight on all his magnificent four legs and walked slowly on his own without any help.

"What we are hoping for" I overheard a commentator say "Is for Shamrocks to recover his colic condition by passing some of the blockage in his colon" so in another word have a big poop!

The vet lead him around and around for what seemed like a couple of hours. Journalists kept calling for a comment but I just ignored them. I was so upset still and yet had a glimmer of hope inside me. Surgery would not be an option, it would take too long to make it to the Royal Equine Hospital in London and by then it could be fatal. Kerry had gone and got hot chocolates for everyone and brought me my wellies and a cardigan. I tried to be grateful but it felt like mums death all over again and this time the whole world was watching. Ted came to check in from time to time but I just ignored him completely.

The vet joked about how many miles he was doing when suddenly Shamrocks stopped. We all watched and hoped he would not collapse onto the cold concrete floor. He gave a huge groan and lifted his tail up high and with that a massive pooh came flopping down to the ground. Our vet punched the air in victory and a big cheer and clapping came from the people who had gathered outside the fence. I ran towards Shamrocks and gave him a huge hug.

"We are out of the woods young Molly. Luckily you saw him last night, I'm afraid he would have been a dead horse by now if you hadn't" said the vet who looked relieved.

"Will he be ok for tomorrow?" I asked.

"He's just survived a huge ordeal, it's far too early to say. It depends on how he gets on today and tonight, I wouldn't advise it to be honest." He said truthfully.

"Ok, thank you so much for everything" I said.

"Thank you, thank you" said my dad shaking his hand firmly.

"Let him rest and offer him a bran mash in about two hours' time, I'll be back to check on him then." And the vet handed me the lead to take over for now. I stayed with him stroking his neck and talking rubbish. I knew Ted had come and gone from next door. Best he keeps his distance, the two timing so and so!

Dad made a bran mash and offered it to Shamrocks, he just sniffed it and turned his nose. When the vet arrived he checked him all over and said as soon as he gets his appetite then he would be much better.

The day passed and night fell upon us again. Shamrocks did not want anything to eat still. It was getting late and I was very tired. I had been up for nearly 48 hours. Dad insisted I go back to bed and he would sleep with Shamrocks for the night. I was so tired when my head hit the wobbly blow up bed pillow. I closed my eyes and fell fast asleep in no time.

I woke up and looked around. Kerry was asleep, no sign of dad, he must be with Shamrocks still. I got dressed and ran as fast as I could to the yard. As I got closer I heard the most magnificent familiar sound. It was little Shamrocks whinny. I ran down the aisle to his stable as he was guzzling into the feed of bran and my dad holding the bucket.

"He's going to be OK! The vet was here earlier and couldn't figure out why he didn't want his food, so we put in his secret ingredient… Guinness, and he's cleaned the bucket nearly!" said dad who looked tired and very happy with himself.

"Will he be ok for today?" I asked hopefully.

"I'm not sure pet, but as long as he's alright that's all the matters" said dad. Shamrocks gave me a huge nudge and I got bran mash and Guinness all over my top… ewe!

Chapter 23

"So the question on everybody's lips today is; will you and Shamrocks be competing in the final for a chance to win Gold?" asked a geeky reporter as I stood in the wings of the grand arena waiting to enter to walk the course. The captain had thought it a good idea for me to walk and learn the course and we would see if the vet gave Shamrocks the all clear.

"It's really down to him now, we've come this far and that's good enough for us" I told the cameras. It was hard to believe that over three million viewers around the world were tuned in to watch the event and yet when you talk into the cameraman it just feels like your talking to someone with a big silly hat on.

"What can you tell us about Shamrocks, does he know how special he is to everyone back in Ireland?" said the commentator.

"No, he's just an average horse, he loves carrots and polo mints and the odd Guinness!" I joked.

"Speaking of polo mints, do you have a

message to send to a Mrs Hegarty who claims Shamrocks ransacked her store?" said the commentator with a smile.

"I'll be sure to warn him" I began to say "to wear a balaclava next time, so she won't recognise him!" The crowd that had gathered around us roared out laughing in amusement.

"And finally Molly, if you win gold today, you're only sixteen years old and your first major championship. Do you have any advice for young equestrians alike out there?" asked the commentator.

I had to think for a moment and then told him, "A wise woman once said: There are only two tragedies in life: one is not getting what one wants, and the other is getting it"

"Was that not Oscar Wilde?" he questioned.

"No, it was Rosie who visits my dad's pub in Clada, 'O'Neil's Bar'" I thought putting a plug in for my dad might be a good idea. Looking over at my dad who was waiting for me to finish, he gave me a thumbs up sign. Just then the Captain came over and told the media that was all for now. We entered into the arena to walk the course, I looked around and the first thing that came into my head was… I'm in Narnia!

The fences were not big, wide or huge.... No, they were bloody enormous, bloody huge and scary wide. I had a sudden gut feeling that maybe it's for the best that Shamrocks is ill, this looks suicide! The Captain walked the course with me and my dad. Every jump was tricky, every angle was tight and then there was the London Dungeons Jump. It was a new obstacle to the Olympic Games, it consisted of a jump in, tunnel underground and jump your way out up the hill over three elements, with spooky objects along the line. All the riders scratched their heads and cursed, re-walked and complained. There were three horrible skulls looking from above over the drop down and riders complained about the spookiness. I wasn't sure if Shamrocks would be spooked but I know I was petrified of them. An added touch was when a rider approached, fire was going to blow from behind the skulls to make the matters even worse!

Ted, Murt, Jessica, Padraig and I all stood in a group as the Captain gave us our final instructions.

"First up for us will be Padraig, then you Murt, then Ted. Jessica you will be next and Molly if Shamrocks is declared you will jump last. The course is not easy. The English have an advantage as it's their home ground and a little birdy has told me that their horses have seen all this before!" The

Captain cleared his throat before continuing, but not before Murt spoke up.

"That's feckin cheating! I demand a rebuild! And we should put in an official complaint!" said Murt.

"It's too late, anyway we've no proof" said the Captain.

"No proof, no feckin proof. The proof will be in the fecking Bronze. Silver and Gold later today!" said Murt. He did have a point in fairness to him.

"Murt will you shut up!" snapped the Captain. "It's rumours, now don't go causing any trouble or I'll kick you off the squad myself"

"What about dope testing" asked Jessica looking at me directly.

"What are you on about Jessica?" asked the Captain getting furious with such unprofessional questions at this time.

"I'm just saying, what if one did get a medal, would their horses be tested?" she queried.

"Yes of course they would. Why? Is there something we need to know right now?" said the

Captain who was looking rather pink in the face.

"No. I'm just asking, Shamrocks has had a lot of stuff in the last twenty four hours, would that not enhance his performance?" she said.

"No, it was recovery medication and has been cleared by an official vet, happy?" asked the captain who got a nod from Jessica. "Right children, any more questions? Because this isn't the time for messing about!" He had raised his voice and some other competitors and trainers looked on and tried to listen in.

"Padraig, you go get ready. The rest of you stay in the Ireland section of the stand so I can keep an eye on you. Murt, absolutely under no circumstances must you have a drink" instructed Captain.

We all sat and talked about the course. I confessed to dad I think it was best that we gave it a miss as it looked too over facing! He agreed and we decided to wait and withdraw Shamrocks near the end of the course as not to let on to any of the other competitors at this time.

Following the first three riders who all had disastrous rounds, it was Padraig's turn. He had a lovely bay gelding with feathered fetlocks and hooves the size of dinner plates. He went plod plod plod to every jump safely until he came to the water jump and landed splash in the middle. It was deep as well as wide and when they came out the other side his front tendon boot was hanging down and causing his gelding to trip, which forced him to pull up. He encored twenty eight time false. It had been the best round to date.

The English riders came in and went out, all knocking, stopping, dunking and refusing to enter the dungeon.

"They must have heard me talk earlier and are now changing their minds" said Murt satisfied with himself.

"Murt, you idiot!, this is the Olympics, I don't think they heard you earlier and I don't think they had done the course already by the looks of things" said Ted who was clearly getting wound up and anxious because he was up next.

"Good Luck" I said to him as he left the stand, he just nodded and made his way down the stand to his horse. I was to watch Ted and Murt and then make my way down to warm up Shamrocks. I was slightly relieved not to be jumping as nobody had made it around the course yet. We didn't tell the captain yet as he seemed to be under a lot of pressure!

At last, it was Ted's turn. I felt nervous for him. Despite the silly mind games he plays with girls I was hoping and wishing he made it around safely. Ted came cantering softly towards the front jump, a little too soft because as his little mare was mid-way in the air her front legs paddled as if trying to make it to the other side but came tumbling and crashing down into the middle of the jump. Ted hit the ground and the crowd groaned and jumped to their feet. He lay still and his little mare galloped away into the middle of the arena. Everyone watched in silence waiting for his limp body to move, suddenly he pushed himself up spitting out dirt from his mouth, a few course attendants gathered and asked did he need paramedics, he brushed himself off and stood up. The crowd applauded with relief that he was ok, he acknowledged by waving at the crowd and exiting the arena joked to the camera "I can't even do the first jump!" I was relieved he was alright but the thoughts of having to ride the course terrified me. Murt was to follow shortly, he was doing a little better than Ted was until he suddenly started to loop the arena and forgot his way, when he suddenly realised he tried to make up some time he had lost and ploughed through a set of jumps, braking poles and sending bits of timber flying in all directions. As I looked down I could see the Captain holding his head in his hand. We weren't exactly the team he had in mind when selecting us, I imagined Patricia the fat lady sat in her big armchair in Northern Ireland shaking her head in disapproval. I then remembered all the sad faces that were in the room when he selected the team. I was part of that team selection. Why was I so frightened and trying to chicken out? As I turned to tell my dad that I should do it, the Captain came running up the steps and to our side.

"Jessica has bailed" he said bluntly.

"What's wrong?" asked my dad in surprise, he had not spoken to Mr Walsh all summer and they simply only passed each other off for politeness.

"Well let's just say… she's a little concerned about a certain test that might be done should she go clear. Not that she would, this course is the worst I have ever come across." said the Captain. "Molly, you ready?" he asked.

"I'm not sure if Shamrocks will be up to it" confessed my dad, not actually saying it was me that was not up to it.

"I've just spoken to the vet, he's happy

Shamrocks is fit and well. Kerry has been baby-sitting all this time, so nobody has even dared step foot near him!" said the Captain.

"Well, I don't know now..." trailed my dad. "It's just I would be worried we could over face him"

"Don't think I haven't considered that Martin?, but I picked your daughter and her horse for one reason and one reason only, now are you going to give her a chance or not?" asked the Captain.

Just then I decided to speak up... or forever hold my bid! "Captain" I began. My dad tried to stop me from talking but I just shushed him and looked at the Captain. "To be honest" I continued "this track is like nothing Shamrocks has ever done" the Captain nodded and looked away, he was realising that any hope of a medal for Ireland was not going to be achieved. But then when I said "But we didn't come here for nothing, so come on... let's give it a go!" He put his arms around me and told me to run as fast I could to get Shamrocks!

Chapter 24

I trotted quickly from the stables through the courtyard towards the path towards the arenas, Shamrocks was full of beans and delighted to be out of his stable after being ill. Kerry was running behind me shouting instructions and panicking.

"I feel sick" I could hear her shout "You'll be fine, nothing to worry about" she was saying and laughing hysterically for no reason at all, "It's just like a small gymkhana back home" who was she trying to kid? I looked over my shoulder and for the first time in my life, shouted at her.

"Kerry shut up, you're making me nervous!" I said. People were moving out of our way as we thundered down the grass laneway as we had no time to spare, I kicked Shamrocks on into a full speed gallop and he raised his tail and pricked his ears forward. He was loving this and so was I, not sure how we would feel in about ten minutes though!

The practice arena was empty. The two riders before us, where queuing up at the pocket to the main arena so this left the practice arena free for me and Shamrocks. My dad and the Captain quickly moved the jumps from the position they were in and told me to jump a few jumps at tight angles rather than straight runs. The media left the main arena as it was old news now when you heard the crowd groan or a clatter of poles as they hit the ground. There was still no clear round and as the media gathered, security was hushing them away out of sight so as not to distract us.

"You know your course?" asked the Captain. I nodded yes. "Watch that first line and remember do not approach it straight, jump it to the right and turn whilst in the air. After that you know what to do, and if he spooks at the skulls…. Well, who could blame him? Good luck my little Molly, I know you'll do your best" as he patted my knee and Shamrocks on the neck and left to watch our round from the viewing tower.

"You nervous pet?" asked my dad.

"Never been better" I lied. He looked straight in my eyes and I couldn't help it but he I felt so emotional I wanted to cry. "She's watching, isn't she dad?" I asked him.

"You bet she is kid, she is so proud of you. You are the bravest little girl… little woman in Ireland right now. You do the best you can and don't be worried if you have any trouble, or just retire if you don't want to go ahead ok" said dad who was also filling up with tears.

"Ok" I snuffled, I had to wipe my runny nose on my jacket. I looked down and giggled.

"You're always scruffy just as you go in... what am I going to do with you?" he joked.

"Molly O'Neil, you're next in twenty seconds" shouted the boy at the gate. Dad held my hand and kissed mums charm bracelet as we walked slowly towards the entrance. There was nothing left to say now. I squeezed his hand whilst the boy opened the massive arena gate shouting "Five... Four... Three... Two... One!" and pointed his index finger signaling for me to enter into the arena. I walked into the arena still clutching dads hand and once we were in I looked around at the magnificent crowd of people. I heard the loudest cheer and roar from the crowd that I had ever heard in my life, I looked at dad for reassurance and he gave me a wink as I let go of his hand and gathered my reins I kicked Shamrocks into the center of the arena. I was instructed to make sure and canter by the bogey jumps, the dungeon, water jump and massive wall. As we rode in, the commentator began announcing our names in English then French and then another language I did not know, maybe Spanish?

After a few seconds the crowd settled down, I kicked Shamrocks into a canter to do a full lap of the arena before starting. Unlike other horses, Shamrocks needed speed so we gathered up our pace as I shortened my reins and kept my eye on the first jump. Just as they Captain had instructed I was to jump the first jump at an angle this made the crowd groan as if I was doing something wrong.. But they didn't know our plan.

"Ok my baby this is it, get around this course and I'll rob Mrs Hegarty's shop for you myself!" I told him. As we approached the first jump, it was a tall upright painted in the union jack flag, we sailed over it at the angle we wanted. Upon landing it was a short four strides to the second. Again I had to kick and gallop him four long strides, his little legs lifted up as high as they possible could go and he cleared number two safely. I could hear the crowd try to keep quiet but the volume of whispering voices was not so silent, I didn't feel alone like I usually did instead I felt encouraged and prayed silently to do well. Fence three was the wall. It was not a traditional red brick wall, instead it had photos of people's faces and made a collage of the Olympic symbol, I had to push kick and gallop. I closed my eyes and shouted at the top of my voice "COME

ON" and again Shamrocks lifted up high as we were landing my seat became unbalanced from the height and my feet slipped from the stirrups and I had to push myself from his neck back into the saddle, the crowd groaned as they were expecting me to hit the dirt! There was no time to waste as we had the water jump next followed by planks. Full throttle we galloped, no rein contact and no time to gather my stirrups back I kicked and pushed like a jockey on a race track as we approached the enormous water jump aka swimming pool! Another scream "COME ON SHAMROCKS" and we stretched wider than ever, I could hear the crowd go wild as we landed the other side. Normally you would steady for the planks, but with Shamrocks we needed to keep the wheels in motion and galloped to the tall planks that looked like a railway crossing. The flashing lights either side did not phase Shamrocks at all, we cleared the planks and alas only had a few more jumps before the final dungeon.

Still clear, is this really happening I thought? No time to think, one last element to go. I turned the corner and looked at the spooky hole we needed to jump into, it now looked a lot more dangerous than I had thought. As we got closer I could see the three skeletons looking at us waiting to explode fire as we approached. I suddenly got an image of the three donkeys that were in the field where I met Shamrocks and the thought made me smile. "How are ye lads?" I shouted in my moment of madness. Shamrocks ears pricked as he enjoyed listening to my voice, perhaps it made him feel not alone too, so I talked some more. "Just one jump to go, don't look left or right...." And as we got closer and about to take off and jump into the tunnel I shouted "Close your eyes Shamrocks" and we went high into the air and upon landing down, down, down and into the darkness of the underground I opened my eyes and said to him "Open them again, or we'll crash" and we rode through the tunnel as we exit we heard the surrounding crowd "Ohh" and "Ahhh" we had one big jump to do. It was from this side of the steep hill and nobody had cleared it to date. Still no stirrups I sat as if we were bareback again and vision the jump as the stone wall we first did when we first met all those months ago. I kicked screamed and pushed, Shamrocks lifted and lifted and lifted. It was like magic and we were floating in the air, I looked down and could see the ground under me travelling by so fast. As we touched down my body landed on his neck, I tried to push myself back into the saddle. It was no good, Shamrocks head was lowering with my weight even he couldn't lift me back on. The crowd all stood to their feet and groaned and cheered. I could see the finish flags, we needed to get through the finish before I fall off or else we would get eliminated. Shamrocks couldn't hold my weight any longer and he slowed down to a trot and then to a walk. I tried to push myself back into the saddle but it was too far away. My body was slipping off the side and I wrapped my legs around his neck. I was literally hanging from his neck. People were shouting and didn't want to look. All we needed was for Shamrocks to walk through the finish beam for us to have a clear round. Because of our speed we had plenty of time to spare but only if he walked forward about four more steps!!

Through the noisy crowd, I closed my eyes and began to feel defeated. There was nothing else I could do and I was starting to feel humiliated. Then I heard a familiar voice…

"Come on Shamrocks" I heard it again.

"Come on darling, I'm over here" It said again. Who was it? Mum?

"Mum?" I mumbled into Shamrocks neck. He lifted his neck slightly and took a step. Then I heard the voice again and he took another step. I looked to my right, I could nearly touch the finish flag... Then I heard the voice once more.

"Come on Sweethearts you can do it" said

the screaming voice and Shamrocks put one foot forward and through the finish beam. Screams went off around the arena, the commentator roared with the exciting news, and my arms could not hold on any longer so I let go and fell to the hard ground taking lumps of poor Shamrocks mane and plaiting bands in my hand. Paramedics came running over. As I caught my breath back I stood up, the commentator was running towards us with a microphone.

"Molly O'Neil, the only clear round and a GOLD for Ireland, how does this make you feel?" He shouted holding the microphone to my face and an earphone in his ear at the same time as trying to ask the questions.

I couldn't answer him, I held onto Shamrocks neck and cried like I've never before into his wet sweaty neck. Crowds of people came running into the arena to congratulate us and I searched for dad. Where was he? Where was Kerry? I shouted out loud "DAD?" and people looked around to try finding him. I tried again "DAD?" then some shouted "He's over here" and the crown parted to make way for us, then when I saw him we ran towards each other at full speed. He lifted me up high and swung me around in circles. "You did it" he said with tears running down his cheeks.

"No.. WE did it" I said.

"And not forgetting the old Donkey!" he cried out, people around us laughed and hugged us in excitement. "Where's Kerry?" he asked frantically looking through the crowd. He began to panic as he couldn't find her anywhere. Still holding me in his arms he looked around thanking fellow friends and good wishers for our success, I knew that all he wanted now was to share our success with Kerry.

"Dad, I think it's time.. " I said smiling to him.

"What do you mean Molly?" he asked as he held my hand still pushing people aside looking for her.

"Time to ask her something!" I said still smiling.

"I don't know what you're on about" he said. We were still rambling through loads of people that it suddenly dawned on me we had left poor Shamrocks standing in the arena!

"Shamrocks!" I shouted and let go of dads hand to run back to Shamrocks side who was happily being photographed eating a full packet of polo mints all in one gulp! As I got closer I realised who was holding Shamrocks all this time. It was Kerry with big smudged black mascara running down her face and Shamrocks slime all over her clothes. She put her arms out to give me a huge hug.

"Your mum would have been so proud of you" she whispered. "I love you" she said crying in my arms.

"I love you too Kerry" I sobbed. "I think my dad's looking for you."

"Sure he probably just wants to tell me to get back to the pub, that the party's over!" she said. Then looking up she saw my dad standing staring at us both.

"Martin" she said shyly. "Congratulations to you both" she tried to wipe the mascara from her eyes and push her hair behind her ears.

"Molly pet" said my dad "Give me one of them plaiting bands from Shamrocks mane will ya"

I was thinking he could have given Kerry a little hug or something. I opened my hand, I was still holding the lump of mane with plaiting bands that I had pulled of Shamrocks neck as I fell after going through the finish line. I took out a white band

and gave it to my dad. He walked slowly towards Kerry never taking his eyes off hers, then he knelt down on one knee and took Kerry's hand, he lifted the plaiting band and asked:

"Kerry Malone, will you do me the greatest honour in my life, and take Molly as your step daughter and me as your husband?"

"Oh my God Ladies and Gentlemen" announced a commentator nearby "It looks like Mr O'Neil is proposing only moments after his daughter has won a Gold medal for Ireland!" Everyone around gasped and waited for an answer. Kerry looked shocked as she looked over at me with her blurry smudged eyes and back to my dad.

"Of course I will" she said kneeling down onto the ground to meet my dad and giving him a very long long kiss as they both hugged each other. The crowd all cheered and their kiss was televised and shown on the huge giant screen over the main arena. The Commentator announced he had never seen a Gold medal win like it.

After we left the arena and sometime later there was the big ceremony. They played the Irish National Anthem and I stood there with a Gold medal around my neck as the Irish flag was raised, Shamrocks with a garland of flowers around his neck, my dad and Kerry holding hands with the white elastic plaiting band around her wedding finger I knew life could not get any better than this… unless they had a baby I thought, how cool would that be!

Epilogue

Life in Clada after our return was never the same. My dad's pub was now a major tourist attraction with people travelling from all over the country to see the Gold Medal that hung proudly behind the bar. Shamrocks even had a visitor slot to accommodate the fans he had established and people all wanting to get their photos taken beside him.

I am pleased to say, I am now a big sister. Kerry and dad eloped to Las Vegas soon after the Olympic Games and a baby soon followed. They have called her Ciara and a black Shetland pony called Jelly Tots has already been purchased which keeps Shamrocks amused.

On our way home from London, there were thousands of people lining the streets to meet Shamrocks and I, rode him down O'Connell Street and passed Smithfield where I grew up with mum.

We stopped at mum's grave, this time dad and Kerry came with me. I left the wreath of flowers that Shamrock wore around his neck after winning and showed her my medal. I knew and felt in my heart that she was with me through the whole journey and

I don't expect she's left me yet. Until I meet her again someday, for now she will always be in my heart and guiding me through my life, for this, I love you mum.

The End

Made in the USA
Charleston, SC
08 December 2012